DISCONNECTED

Shelley Hrdlitschka

ORCA BOOK PUBLISHERS

Canadian Cataloguing in Publication Data
Hrdlitschka, Shelley, 1956 –
Disconnected

ISBN 1-55143-105-X
I. Title.
PS8565.R44D57 1998   jC813'.54   C98-910782-5   PZ7.H853Di 1998

Library of Congress Catalog Card Number: 98-85661

Orca Book Publishers gratefully acknowledges the support of our publishing programs provided by the following agencies: the Department of Canadian Heritage, The Canada Council for the Arts, and the British Columbia Arts Council.

Cover design by Christine Toller
Cover painting by Ljuba Levstek
Printed and bound in Canada

Orca Book Publishers
PO Box 5626, Station B
Victoria, BC Canada
V8R 6S4

Orca Book Publishers
PO Box 468
Custer, WA   USA
98240-0468

98 99 00   5 4 3 2 1

To Peter, for making my dream possible.

Acknowledgements

My heartfelt thanks to my daughters Danielle, Cara and Kyla for their constant enthusiasm and support; the members of my writing group, past and present, for keeping me on course with their never-ending nagging and nitpicking but especially for their wise advice and encouragement; Alice Frampton, Laura Doolan and Rev. Brian Kiely who read this book in its first draft and whose useful suggestions were a huge help; Jonathan Frampton and Robert Dahling for their thumbs-up approval of the book; and Andrew Wooldridge of Orca Books who skillfully succeeded in making my first experiences with an editor and the editing process completely painless, easy and enjoyable.

He felt strong as he pulled himself through the salty water. Left arm, right arm, left arm, right arm. A perfect flutter kick. He headed straight out from shore. The urge to escape was overwhelming. It was the only thing to do. Leave it all behind. Left arm, right arm, left arm, right arm. Kick. Kick. His body torpedoed smoothly through the lapping waves.

The rhythm of the motion lulled him. The water felt warm and comforting, as if he were wrapped in protective arms. But he had to press on. Had to get away. Had to fight the urge to let the warm water pull him down, down to the ocean floor where he could float, drifting with the ocean currents.

....

"Rise and shine Tanner. Breakfast is on the table." Tanner's mom pulled open the blinds before hustling out of his room and down the hall. Tanner opened his eyes slowly, adjusting to the light in his room. Damn, he thought. He'd had it again. The swimming dream. The dream where he was hell-bent on escaping something. But what was it? What did he want to escape from so badly? He shook his head, trying to clear it.

The funny thing was he didn't even know how to swim, but it came to him so easily in the dream.

"Tanner!"

His mother's voice, hollering from the kitchen, snapped him back to the present. He threw off the covers and pulled on his faded, oversized jeans. He yanked his favorite Edmonton Oilers T-shirt over his head. Stopping briefly in the bathroom on his way to the kitchen, he tried to comb flat the clump of hair that always stood straight up right at the crown of his head. As usual, no amount of water did the trick, so he rubbed a little of Nicole's gel between his hands and smoothed it over the wayward hairs. There, he thought. That should do it.

"Your dad and I have some errands to run today, honey." Tanner's mom ladled some scrambled eggs onto his plate as she talked. His dad and Nicole were already eating. "We need to pick up a few more things for tonight's dinner. Have you made plans for today?"

"No, just hangin' out, I guess." Tanner kept his eyes averted. He could sense his mom's energy and didn't want to get drawn into her agenda. He didn't share her love of mornings but came alive late at night when she was winding down.

"Just make sure you're here in plenty of time for dinner, son." Tanner's dad lowered the newspaper he was reading and studied Tanner. His eyes were gentle, taking in Tanner's not-yet-quite-awake appearance, but his voice was serious. "The whole fam-damily will be here tonight, and we expect some help from you two."

"I'll help with Baby Kyle," said Nicole, looking excited. "And then Lindsay can help you, mom." Lindsay was Tanner and Nicole's older sister. She was married to Kirk and had recently given birth to Baby Kyle, as everyone called him. They were driving up to Edmonton from their home in Red Deer for Thanksgiving dinner.

"I don't think so," grumbled Tanner. He pronounced each word slowly. "If I have to work, so do you. Playing with a baby ain't work." He looked at his sister with narrowed brown eyes, taking in her rumpled appearance. Her long blond hair was matted from sleep and she had yet to apply the usual thick layer of mascara that accented her large blue eyes.

"Is too! Do you want to change his diaper? Do you want to feed him?"

"Not likely! But those things aren't work for you. I'll serve drinks, you can do the dishes. That's fair." She was such an easy target. He loved watching her get steamed.

"I'm in charge of assigning jobs." Tanner's dad ended the argument. "And there won't be any bickering at the table to-night, right?" He looked from one to the other, waiting for eye contact and a nod from each. At thirteen, Nicole was only a year younger than Tanner and he couldn't remember a time when they had actually got along. His dad continued. "Now, Tanner, you're to clean up the breakfast dishes before you get busy 'hangin' out,' and Nicole, you're to do something about that garbage dump you call your room. When your mom and I get back, I want to be able to walk through it without risking my neck."

....

Tanner stood at the kitchen sink watching the bubbles rise as the tap water flowed in. His thoughts moved back to the dream he'd had again last night. It was the same dream he'd had at least a dozen times over the past year and now he was having it even more frequently. There was something very disturbing about it. The actual dream wasn't bad. The swimming felt good and the decision to leave something behind felt right. But something was very wrong ... He felt the dull throb of a headache coming on.

The sensation of water around his feet dropped Tanner back to the present. He quickly turned off the tap and mopped up the puddle. Reaching for the griddle he gently slid it into the mound of soapy water. He ran the washcloth up and down its smooth surface.

Anger. That's what it was. He felt so much anger when he woke up from the dream. But he didn't know who or what he was angry at. He pulled the plug in the sink and dried his hands on a tea towel. He'd let the dishes air dry and put them away later, before his dad got home. Right now he had to sit down. The pain in his head was intense.

Tanner sat on the living room couch and held his head between his hands. The pounding was excruciating, driving out all thoughts of the dream, as well as everything else. He didn't hear the ringing of the phone, nor did he notice the lamp on the end table as it trembled ever so gently.

Leaning on the counter as he bit into his sandwich, Alex looked out at the quiet town. He was in charge of the family service station today while his mother was in the adjoining house, preparing their Thanksgiving dinner. His dad was ... well, who knew where his dad was. Only the pumps were open today. The shop was closed. Alex suspected he was at the pub, his dad's usual refuge when he wasn't in the shop.

Jingle jingle. The sound of a car pulling up to a gas pump forced Alex to abandon his lunch to attend to the customer.

"What will it be today, Mr. Steel?" Alex could turn on the charm, even when he least felt like it. He had been pumping gas and acting charming for years.

"Fill it up please. You can check under the hood and don't forget to wash the windows."

"Certainly, sir. Right away, sir." Alex wondered if Mr. Steel could hear the sarcasm, just barely disguised under the cloak of good manners.

Two more cars pulled in and Alex gave up hope of ever getting back to his sandwich. He pulled up his collar to keep out the damp ocean breeze. He pumped gas, washed windows, checked oil. His lips were curved up in a polite smile, but that smile didn't reach his eyes.

Finally there was a break in the stream of customers. He went back into the station and finished his lunch. He opened the *Vancouver Sun* to the Employment Opportunities section and became so absorbed in it that he didn't see the car that pulled up to the house instead of the pumps. He jumped when the bell over the door jangled.

"Hey, Alex. How goes it?" Alex's Uncle Don stood there grinning at him, his hands busy smoothing down the wind-blown wisps of hair that were grown long to comb over the bald spot on top. Alex was struck once again by how much his uncle looked like his dad.

"Hey, Uncle Don." Alex returned the greeting with less enthusiasm. The party had started. "Dad's out, and Mom's in the house. You're the first to arrive."

"Well you know what they say, son. The early worm gets the bird — or in this case, the turkey I guess!" He laughed loudly at his own joke while Alex smiled politely. It was going to be a long evening.

....

Alex took his time closing up the shop. When he entered the house the party was in full swing. The other guests had arrived, and the house was thick with cigarette smoke. The voices were loud and quarrelsome so Alex knew the drinking had started too. He slipped into the kitchen where his mom was basting the turkey.

"Hi honey. Busy day?"

"Steady." He watched as she struggled with the roasting pan, trying to push it to the back of the ancient oven. A lock of hair had fallen into her eyes and she smoothed it into place with the oven mitt that covered her hand.

"Business was steady or I should be steady?" she asked, removing the oven mitts and reaching for a glass of wine. He noticed how bleary-eyed she looked already. He wondered if it was from the wine or just fatigue.

"Both, I guess. How long till dinner?"

"About half an hour. You better go say hi to everyone, and then hit the shower."

Alex took a deep breath and then pushed open the swinging door to the living room. He looked around at the familiar faces of his dad's relatives; his mom's family lived on the mainland. His Aunt Reggie pulled her great bulk out of the chair and rushed across the room to give him a hug.

"My, you've grown," she declared. Alex smiled politely, wondering why she couldn't think of something more original to say. How would she feel if he said the same thing to her each time they got together?

"How old are you now? Let's see, did you turn thirteen or fourteen on your last birthday?"

"Fourteen," he replied as he reached to shake his Uncle Sam's outstretched hand. He moved around the room, greeting the remaining relatives. As soon as he could without being rude, he excused himself and headed down the hall to his room. After shutting and locking the door behind him, he pulled a wad of bills out of the pocket of his jeans and counted them. Then he reached up and removed a large trophy from his bookshelf. Turning it upside down he pulled back the felt bottom. He quickly shoved the wad of bills up into the hollow center of the trophy, replaced the felt and returned the trophy to its spot on the bookshelf.

There's almost enough, he thought. A few more weeks should do it.

.... three

Sandwich in one hand, TV remote in the other, Tanner flicked through the stations, looking for a sports program. A couple of Tylenol had fixed his headache, and he was ready to eat again. When the phone rang, he reached back and pulled it off the wall, his eyes never leaving the screen.

"Tanner."

"Jason. What's up."

"Not much. I called you earlier. No one answered. You out?"

"No. I've been here all day." He continued to flick through the stations as they talked.

"Maybe I called the wrong number."

"Must have." A picture of crashing waves appeared on the TV screen. Tanner froze. His thumb moved away from the channel advancer. He watched the gulls as they screeched and dove. Tidal pools dotted the vast, deserted beach. Beyond the sand there was nothing but open ocean and gray blue sky meeting on the horizon. This was the same scene that had appeared in his dreams countless times.

"Hey, Tanner. You there?"

"Yeah yeah." Tanner had never been within five hundred kilometers of the ocean, but just by watching the scene on TV he could smell the salt and decaying seaweed. He knew what the ocean would taste like on his lips and how it would leave a gritty film on his skin.

"I'm going down to Rundle Park. Could be our last chance to skate for a while. Snow's supposed to come tomorrow. You comin'?"

Tanner paused, his eyes still glued to the TV. The camera was following the path of some crabs scuttling along the beach. He'd been there in his dream. He knew the feel of the sea spray on his face and how deep his bare feet would sink into the sand when the waves crashed over them. He shuddered and turned the TV off.

"Sure. Just gotta finish my lunch. Meet you there in fifteen."

Tanner put his plate in the dishwasher and poked at the defrosting turkey in the sink. The sight of it spurred him into action. He'd better be gone when his parents returned or they'd rope him into helping prepare for the Thanksgiving invasion.

He maneuvered his skateboard along the city streets, ignoring the looks of the pedestrians as he wound his way toward the skateboard bowl. He felt a twinge of guilt, knowing it was illegal to skateboard on the sidewalk, but he was in control. Besides, he thought, they didn't own the road, or the sidewalk for that matter.

....

An hour later, Tanner and Jason were sprawled out on the grassy bank, catching their breath. They watched the other boarders perform their stunts. Tanner pulled off his toque, trying to cool off. Jason glanced at him.

"Toque head!" he laughed. "You should see yourself."

"You don't look so great yourself, and when did you last take a shower?"

"Just trying to clear some room in the bowl, man. You should try it."

"Yeah, right," answered Tanner. Jason had been his best friend since kindergarten. In the past they'd been able to talk about anything, but lately it was getting more awkward. There were so many changes. Jason always looked okay. He wore a little gold ring in his ear and his complexion was clear. His hair was always neatly pulled back into a ponytail. But he could use a daily shower.

"Do you dream much, Jase?"

"Yeah, I guess. The usual." He glanced at Tanner and then smiled. "Are you talking about the dreams you have in your sleep or fantasies?"

"I know about your fantasies, Jason." Tanner smiled as he remembered the night they'd stayed up late swapping day-dreams. They had discussed their dream cars, dream homes and dream women. As it got later the fantasies got more de-tailed and Tanner's dad eventually had to tell them to can the laughter and get some sleep.

"No, I'm talking about night dreams. The kind you have when you're asleep."

"Well, yeah. Everyone dreams. What about it?"

"Have you ever had one that you've had before?"

"The same dream twice?"

"Or more than twice. Lots of times."

"Now that's weird. No I haven't. And I've never heard of anyone else having rerun dreams either. Why? Have you?"

"Yeah."

"What's it about? Madonna?" Jason laughed at his own joke. Tanner smiled.

"Believe it or not, I'm swimming away from something.

It's almost like a nightmare but not quite. I don't know why I keep getting it."

"No, I don't believe it. You don't even know how to swim. Maybe you're crackin' up, man." Jason reached over and placed a hand on Tanner's forehead. "Nope. No fever. It's confirmed. You're crackin' up. Time to see a shrink." Jason laughed and pushed his skateboard toward the dip. "Better do some more skating, man, before you're committed." He laughed as he rolled away. Tanner followed, disappointed that Jason didn't take him seriously, but not surprised. He'd never heard of anyone having rerun dreams either.

....

Tanner pushed his plate away. He was stuffed. He watched as Lindsay, his older sister, tried to bounce her baby on her lap and eat her turkey dinner at the same time. The baby was fussing but everyone else was still eating.

"Want me to take him for a minute, Lindsay?"

Lindsay looked at Tanner, surprised.

"Thanks, Tanner. I'd really appreciate it."

Tanner reached across the table for his nephew and then propped the baby up in front of him. He looked intently into the little face.

"Hey little buddy. Don't you know big boys don't cry? What's the matter anyway? Your mom won't give you a turkey bone to chew on?"

Kyle stopped fussing and watched Tanner, wide-eyed. This was a different voice, a different face. It gave him something to think about.

"I'll take him now Tanner. I'm finished." Nicole, Tanner's younger sister, leaned over, reaching for the baby.

"Can't you see we're having a heart-to-heart talk here, Nicole? You can have him when he starts crying again." Tanner put his face up to the baby's once more. "Now you gotta watch out for that Aunt Nicole, Kyle. She's a wicked one. There's a wicked witch in every family and your Aunt Nicole is ours."

"Tanner. That's enough." Tanner could hear the warning tone in his father's voice.

Tanner decided to change the topic. "So, are you going to grow up big and strong like your Uncle Tanner, Kyle?" The baby's bottom lip stuck out and began to quiver. "Here you go Nicole. Quick. He's all yours." Tanner passed the baby to his younger sister who was seated beside him, but he kept studying the baby's face. He looked around the table at his family and assorted relatives. There was his grandmother, his mom's mother. Then there was his dad's brother, Uncle John, and his wife, Auntie Sue. He looked back at Baby Kyle.

"You know, I think he looks like me. Lindsay, Nicole and Kirk are all blue-eyed. But Kyle has brown eyes like mine." Tanner rubbed the fuzz on the top of the baby's head. "And I bet he gets brown hair like mine, too."

Tanner felt the tension that suddenly filled the room. He looked up to see everyone staring at him, uneasily. They each looked away when he caught their eye. He saw the look that passed between his mom and dad. What had he said wrong?

"As long as he doesn't get your twisted personality, Tanner," said Nicole, rocking the baby in her arms. "There's no room for two of you in this family."

four

Standing in his bedroom with a towel wrapped around his waist, Alex pulled open his closet door and yanked a clean pair of jeans off the shelf. He glanced at the row of crisp, carefully ironed dress shirts hanging there. Beside them, on another shelf, was a stack of cozy sweatshirts. He had a decision to make. Should he please himself and put on a comfortable sweatshirt or should he break down and put on the stiff dress shirt that his father would expect him to wear to their Thanksgiving dinner? If he chose the former there would be the inevitable scene with his father, even if the living room was full of guests. But if he wore the dress shirt he would be giving in, and for the last six months or so he had stopped giving in to his father's attempts to control him. There had been one confrontation after another, but at least he was finally standing up for himself. Tonight, though, he felt tired and somewhat defeated already. Dinner was going to be trying, what with all the relatives that were present, and he just wanted to get it over with so he could meet Cara afterward. He sighed and pulled a shirt off a hanger.

"Yep, ten more years till retirement and then I'm out of

here," his father was saying when Alex joined his relatives in the living room. "Moving to the city. And I won't be back."

"City life's not all it's cracked up to be, Frank." Uncle Tom had worked in Vancouver for a few years. "There's the pollution, the traffic, just the busy-ness of it all. I give you a year and you'll come running back here with your tail tucked firmly between your legs."

"I don't think so. Pat and I are going to attend the theater, try out a new restaurant every week and act like tourists for the rest of our lives. The natural beauty of a town like Tahsis can only sustain a man for so long."

"I'll drink to that," said Uncle Don and they all clinked glasses over the coffee table.

Alex's dad looked around the room. "Who needs another drink? Alex, go get the bottle off the buffet and I'll pour the drinks in here."

....

After dinner, Alex quietly excused himself and began cleaning the mess in the kitchen. He worked hard, keeping one eye on the clock. Cara was going to meet him near the park at eight o'clock. When he was done, he grabbed his coat off the hook and slipped out the door.

The fresh air felt wonderful. The night was clear and an almost full moon illuminated the small town. He drew in a deep breath and headed toward the small restaurant that stood at the outskirts of West Bay Park. Cara was waiting for him. He felt the usual pang deep inside when he saw her. She was standing with her back to the park, peering into the dark, watching for him. The breeze blew her long brown hair forward. Her smile was beautiful, her gray eyes looking so alive.

Alex took her hand gently. She always seemed so delicate. "Want to walk?"

"Sure. I've just got an hour though. I have to be home by nine."

They walked in silence for a few minutes. Alex wondered at what point their relationship had changed. They had known each other since they were very young. They had been two of the ten children who had started kindergarten together. They had always been friends, but sometime in the last year their feelings had changed. He looked down at her as they walked. She was the only thing he was going to miss about this town, but as soon as he had established a new life she could join him.

"I've almost got enough to go," he told her. "I paid myself another thirty dollars today."

She stopped walking and looked up at him. "Alex, why can't you wait a couple more years? Until you've graduated. You'll have a much better chance at getting a job and I could go with you."

"My dad will have caught on to me by then. I'm surprised he hasn't already. He's such a greedy jerk."

"He may be stingy, but two wrongs don't make a right. Stealing from him isn't the answer you know."

"Cara, I thought you were the one person who understood." He dropped her hand and walked down to where the waves lapped at the shore. It was a calm night, and Alex picked up a rock and threw it as hard as he could.

Cara came up behind him and put both hands around his waist. She pulled him close to her. "You know I do, but I think there must be a better way."

Alex swung around, glaring down at her. "You should have heard my dad tonight. He was rattling on again about how he was going to get out of this town the day he retires. Can you believe him? He's worked in this dead-end town all his life. He could get cancer next year and be dead before he retires. What good will his dreams be then? No. I've learned from his mistakes. I'm going to follow my dreams now, and if I have to take money from him to do it then I will. You know he's never paid me a red cent for pumping gas."

"He feels he's doing the right thing," Cara reminded him. "And I don't think it's a dead-end town," she added quietly.

"Oh yeah, sure." Alex used a low voice, imitating his father. "This is going to be your business one day, son. Why should I pay you wages now when I'm going to give you the whole business eventually?"

"When did you last tell him how you felt?"

"That's not the point. He didn't understand before. He won't understand now." Alex imitated his father again. "I've worked long and hard to make this business a success, Alex. You're going to get it handed to you on a silver platter. I won't hear any more talk about following your dreams. You're my only son and you should thank your lucky stars that I've done all this for you." Alex whispered, pleading for Cara to understand. "I can't get out of here fast enough, Cara. I don't want to turn out like the rest of my family."

Cara took both of his hands before answering him. "You won't, Alex. But it's got nothing to do with running away. You're different than them. You're deeper, somehow. Whatever you do with your life, you'll never turn out like them."

Alex studied Cara. She sounded so much older than she was. Her eyes reflected a depth of character that bewildered him.

The honking sounds from a flock of Canada geese landing on the water brought them back to the present. Cara squinted to see her watch in the dark.

"I've got to go. But promise me you'll think some more about this thing, Alex."

He shook his head sadly. "It's a done deal, Cara. I'm leaving. The sooner the better."

Hand in hand, they walked back the way they had come, a heavy mood looming over them. When they reached the restaurant, Alex clutched both of Cara's shoulders and turned her to look at him.

"This is not going to end us, Cara. We'll get through it. You'll wait for me?"

Tears filled her eyes, but she nodded. "You know I will. As long as it takes."

"Thanks." As he hugged her, he could feel her shaking under her winter coat. He didn't know if it was from the cold, or from fear – the fear of losing each other.

five

"You're a disgrace. A no-good. I should have known you'd amount to nothing. It's probably in your genes, your blood." An arm came up — ready to strike.

The anger was overwhelming. He fled. He reached the beach and dove into the water. He was swimming again. It felt right. It felt good. The cool water relieved the hot anger. The steady rhythm of the strokes soothed him. Maybe he would just rest for a moment, sink down to the ocean floor, the untroubled, calm womb of the universe ...

....

The jangling of the alarm clock pulled Tanner out of his troubled sleep. He rolled over and hit the off button. 5:00 a.m. Ugh. Monday morning hockey practice. He scrambled out of bed and quickly pulled on some clothes. He ran his hands through his hair as he entered the dark, silent kitchen. With his fingers wrapped around a large glass of orange juice he sat at the kitchen table, trying to pull himself out of the fuzzy sleep zone he was still in. The swimming dream had changed, he thought. Now he had a hint of what he was running from.

He shuddered. How could he turn these dreams off?

Tanner looked around. Something was different this morning. The house was quiet and cold and there was a pile of dishes on the counter waiting to go into the dishwasher. The smell of turkey still lingered in the air. But it was more than that. The world felt still somehow.

Tanner pulled back the living room curtains so he could watch the street for Jason and his dad who were on their way over to drive him to practice. In the glow of the streetlight he could see snow falling, thick and heavy. No wonder the morning seemed especially peaceful, he thought. The ground was already covered with a deep layer. He watched it, savoring the moment. By the time he got home from practice there would be tire tracks and footprints everywhere, spoiling the pristine beauty of the morning.

When Tanner saw the headlights approaching his house he went downstairs to step into his boots and grab the hockey bag that he had packed the night before. He slipped outside and looked up, feeling the snowflakes touch his face and melt. He felt the tension of the dream fade away. He wished he could skip practice this morning and just enjoy the snow. He sighed and tromped down the stairs.

....

"Listen up, guys. The tournament in Vancouver is just nine weeks away. I'm not taking a mediocre team all the way to the coast. I know you guys are good players — that's why you're on this team. But you've got to use your heads out there. Think!"

Tanner's mind drifted as he listened to the coach talk. Nine weeks seemed like such a long time to wait. It would be his first trip with this team and his first time to the coast.

"So get out there and hustle. Show some intensity."

Tanner felt strong as he skated across the smooth surface of the ice. Jason passed him the puck as he crossed the blue line and headed for the net. He out-maneuvered the first defenseman and looked up to see who he could pass to. The right wing was open. He passed it perfectly. Blake wound up and one-timed the puck into the top left-hand corner of the net. What a goal! What an assist! A perfect play.

The whistle blew and the hockey players gathered around the coach.

"Good work, Tanner, Blake. That's using your heads. I hope the rest of you are taking notes."

Tanner felt his face flush. He was finally proving himself to his new team. It had been an honor to be selected for the Rep team, but when he began to practice with them he'd found the skill level so high that he wondered if he'd be able to keep up. As he turned to skate away he found Edward blocking his path. He tried to skate around him, but Edward stepped sideways to block the way again.

"Punk," he hissed, "you better watch your back." He shoulder checked Tanner and then turned sharply and skated away.

Tanner glanced at the coach, but his attention was elsewhere. When Tanner was sitting on the bench a few minutes later, Jason slid in next to him.

"What's with Edward?" Tanner asked quietly.

Jason's eyes followed the play on the ice, but he answered. "Big Eddy? Is he giving you trouble?"

"No, not really. Just wanted to know what he's like. He didn't like my assist."

"No, I guess that wouldn't make him happy." This was Jason's second year on the Rep team so he knew the other players. "Edward barely made it back on the team this year, so a new guy like you is a real threat to him."

"What's his problem?"

"Who knows. Drugs, probably, judging by the guys he hangs with. Watch out for him. He's got a mean streak, and he's a big guy. You don't want to mess with him or his buddies."

"I hear ya. Don't worry."

....

Glancing at Edward in the locker room, Tanner noticed the muscular frame, the wide shoulders and the ease in his movements. This was a guy who'd taken weight training seriously, he thought. Why would a guy like Edward abuse his body? He couldn't relate.

Jack Freeman, or Mr. Jack, as the players called him, poked his head out of the coaching office that was in the back corner of the locker room.

"Tanner, can I see you for a second? In here."

"Sure." Tanner smacked Jason on the back as he walked by him. "I'll meet you at the front door. If my dad's there, tell him I'm coming."

"Right," said Jason and retaliated by whipping Tanner's back with his towel.

When Tanner entered the little office, the coach was sitting behind his desk. He motioned for Tanner to sit in the chair across from him.

"You made some good moves out there today, Tanner. Not bad for a rookie."

"Thanks."

"I'm doing some line changes. I thought I'd put you on the first line with Jason and Craig."

"Really?" Tanner was surprised. He expected to spend his first year warming the bench. "Isn't that Edward's position?"

"Well, it has been." A frown crossed the coach's face. "But we've been having some trouble with Edward. I'm not sure his heart's in it. Besides, this is just temporary. If Edward wants the spot back, he has to prove it. He's got the ability. He just needs to get his priorities straight."

When Tanner left the coach's office the locker room was almost empty, but Edward was still there, sitting on a bench by the door waiting for a friend. Tanner packed his gear into his bag and headed down the long, narrow corridor. He could feel Edward's eyes on him. Just as he reached the exit, Edward stood up, blocking his path. He towered above Tanner.

"What'd Mr. Jack want, Bolton?"

"Not much. Said he liked my skating today. Could you move it, please?"

Edward glanced in the direction of the coach's office before he snarled, "Don't go thinking any little punk is going to bump me off this team, Bolton. I got friends, you know. And accidents have been known to happen."

"Say what?" Tanner couldn't believe what he was hearing. It was like something from a gangster movie, he thought. Edward must really be losing it.

Edward took a step closer to Tanner. Tanner stood his ground, looking Edward squarely in the eye. He could feel his anger building. He wasn't going to let this guy intimidate him.

"I said move it. I'd like to get by."

Edward just stared at Tanner, a smirk on his face.

"Let me through." Tanner started to push past Edward, but stopped when Edward's friend showed up.

"C'mon you guys," Tanner urged. "Mr. Jack is still in his office. What do you think you're trying to prove?"

"We're trying to prove that you're a nobody, Bolton, and you've got to remember that."

Tanner felt a cold sweat break out. He didn't think he could control his temper much longer. He clenched his fists and was about to force his way between the two when a tremendous crash came from the far end of the locker room. All three boys jumped, and Tanner swung around to see what had happened just as Mr. Jack came out of his office. They all stared at the clutter of empty pop cans lying on the floor.

"How did that happen?" asked the coach. The rack for empty pop cans that stood beside the vending machine lay on its side, and the cans were strewn everywhere.

The three boys just shrugged their shoulders. There wasn't anyone near that end of the room.

"Well don't just stand there. Get over here and help me pick them up."

When Tanner finally got out to the car where Jason was waiting with his father, his mood was grim.

"What did Mr. Jack want?" asked Jason.

"Nothing."

"What do you mean, nothing? He never wants nothing."

"Today he wanted nothing. Okay?"

Jason exchanged a look with Tanner's dad. They recognized the tone in Tanner's voice. There was no point pursuing the conversation. When Tanner didn't want to talk, he didn't. Plain and simple. They drove home through the falling snow in silence.

.... six

The phone on the wall jangled.

"I've got it," called Cara, putting her spoon down beside her bowl of oatmeal.

"Hello?"

"Hello. Cara?"

"Yes."

"This is Pat Swanson, Alex's mom."

Cara froze. She could hear the tension in Mrs. Swanson's voice and she was afraid to hear what the woman had to say.

"I'm sorry to call so early, Cara, but I'm trying to locate Alex. He was gone when we got up this morning. I'm checking in with all his friends to see if they know where he is."

So that's it, thought Cara. He's gone and done it already.

"No, I don't know," she replied. She wondered if Alex's mom could tell she was lying. Actually, she didn't know where Alex was. She just knew that he was planning to leave. So she wasn't really lying, was she?

"When did you last see him?"

Cara paused before she answered. It was just last night that she had gone for a walk with him. She hadn't realized he was planning to leave so soon. He said he had "almost" enough money. She thought that meant it would be a while yet.

"I saw him last night after dinner," she answered honestly. "I went home at nine o'clock so that's when I last saw him."

"He didn't mention where he might be going this morning, early?"

"No." Cara felt sick, and a little angry at Alex. The anguish in Mrs. Swanson's voice was heartbreaking. She wasn't the most with-it mother in the world, but she loved Alex. Living with Mr. Swanson all these years had probably worn her down. And it wasn't his mom that Alex had a problem with, but she was the one getting hurt and Cara was being forced to lie, or at least to cover up the truth.

"Well, if you hear from him, will you let me know?" Mrs. Swanson cleared her throat. "He had a little quarrel with his dad last night and I'm worried that he might still be angry."

"Oh," Cara replied, now understanding why he left so suddenly. "Sure. I'll let you know."

"Thanks." Mrs. Swanson paused again before she continued. Cara could hear a tremor in her voice. "I'm afraid he may have run away."

Cara hung up the phone and slipped down the hall to her bedroom. She closed the door behind her and flopped down on the bed. He's gone, she thought. He really did it. She stared at the ceiling for a long time, letting the feelings of loss and sorrow wash over her.

.... seven

"So you're going on a road trip, eh?"

"Yeah." Tanner sat on the doctor's examining table, naked except for his underwear. The doctor was giving him the required physical exam before he could travel with the team.

"You're on a Rep team. What position do you play?" The doctor warmed the stethoscope before he put it on Tanner's chest.

"Left wing."

"Left wing, hmm. Good, good. How old are you now?"

"Fourteen."

"That's right. Fourteen. Hmm." He looked in each of Tanner's ears and then felt the glands behind them. Satisfied, he sat back on his stool and made some notes in his file.

"Everything looks fine, Tanner. We'll have to run some routine blood and urine tests at the lab, but I don't think we're going to find anything unusual." He looked up from his scribbling and whipped off his glasses. "Is there anything you'd like to discuss now that you're here? Any aches, pains I should know about? Any questions about puberty?"

Tanner groaned to himself. Why did grown-ups always want to talk about puberty? But there *was* something bothering him. Tanner hesitated. He didn't want to disclose any information that might jeopardize his chance to travel with the team, but his headaches were getting worse. He decided to take a chance.

"I get these really bad headaches."

"Uh huh." The doctor put on his glasses again and made a note in the file. "Have you had your eyes checked recently?"

"Yeah. Just a couple weeks ago."

"Show me where these headaches are."

"They're all over. A whole-head thing."

"It could be migraine. Especially if they're severe. What do you do when you get these headaches?"

"I take a couple of Tylenol. It usually numbs the pain."

"Hmm. Tylenol doesn't usually do much for a migraine. Can you think of anything that might trigger your headaches?"

As a matter of fact, Tanner knew exactly what triggered the headaches. It was the swimming dream. But would the doctor think he was crazy if he told him? Again he decided to take a chance.

"Actually, there is a kind of pattern," said Tanner, trying to choose his words carefully. "I've been having this same dream over and over. In the dream I'm swimming away from something. The next morning I always get the headache." He watched the doctor for his reaction. The doctor was studying him, a puzzled expression on his face. He began to flip through Tanner's file again.

"How long have you been getting these dreams and headaches?"

"For a couple of years," he answered, "but I get them all the time now."

"Really." He was reading something in Tanner's file. "I've never heard of dreams triggering headaches before, but there is a first for everything." He paused, lost in thought. "Do you think that if you had someone you could talk to about these dreams it might help the headaches go away?"

"You mean like a shrink? Forget it. I'm not crazy. Forget I said anything about it." Tanner jumped down from the examining table and reached for his clothes that were hanging over the back of the chair.

"Talking to a psychologist doesn't mean you're crazy, Tanner. Absolutely not." The doctor sounded apologetic. "But if it's the dreams that are triggering the headaches, then it's the dreams that we have to deal with."

Tanner had pulled on his clothes and was lacing up his boots. He looked up at the doctor from the chair. "Forget I said anything about it. It's no big deal."

Dr. Thompson looked discouraged. "If you change your mind, come and see me, okay?"

"I won't — change my mind that is. Are you going to fail me on my physical exam?"

"No, of course not. I don't think this is a physical problem."

"Good."

"Is your mom in the waiting room, Tanner?"

"Yeah, why?"

"I want to talk to her about your headaches, just so she is aware of the situation. You can stay and listen if you like."

Although Tanner would have preferred keeping his mother in the dark about his headaches, he felt he had won the battle about seeing a shrink, so he nodded his head. "You talk to her. I need some fresh air."

Pacing the sidewalk a few minutes later, Tanner glanced at his watch. How long could it take the doctor to tell her about his headaches? It was no big deal. The doctor said so himself. Maybe he was talking his mom into taking him to a shrink.

He leaned against the wall of the medical building, trying

to get out of the wind. He pulled his jacket closer around him and tucked his hands under his armpits. He watched the cars driving by, throwing mud-colored slush onto the sidewalk.

Maybe he *was* going crazy, he thought. That dream was making him crazy. It certainly wasn't a normal dream, the kind of dream triggered by something that was happening in his life. It was as if the swimmer wasn't actually him. He felt somehow removed from the feelings, as if he was just looking into someone else's dream. As if someone else's dream had somehow got into his head.

The bell on the door to the medical building tinkled. Tanner glanced over, expecting to see his mom, but it was another kid and his mother. A normal kid with a normal life ...

Disconnected. That was it. He felt disconnected from the swimmer, but connected in an inexplicable way. In fact, he felt somehow cut off from his whole life, dreaming or awake. He'd always had a feeling there was something missing. Not something material, like skis or a bike, but a part of him.

Tanner started stamping his feet. He was getting cold. Where was his mother? It was already getting dark and he was getting hungry. How could they still be talking about him? How long did it take to say your son is getting headaches? Of course, it would take a little longer to say your son is getting headaches that always follow a dream he has about swimming. He doesn't know how to swim, you say? He couldn't take swimming lessons because he always got ear infections? Well, that's strange now, isn't it? I recommend you take him to a psychologist. I do believe your son is going crazy.

Tanner moved back into the lobby to keep from freezing. He slumped into a chair and watched the people milling about the pharmacy on the other side of the lobby. If only he could get a prescription for anti-dream pills, then the headaches would go away. Maybe he had always been crazy. How could he be missing something? He was all there. Two arms, two legs, a body and a head. He had once thought it was a feeling that all kids shared, but when he had tried to talk to Jason about it, Jason just thought he was weird.

Tanner could hear his mom coming before he could see her. Her heels had that determined click about them as she came down the corridor and around the corner to the lobby. He studied her face before she could spot him. Not good. Her forehead was crinkled and she had a faraway look in her eye that meant she was deep in thought. He stood up.

"What took you so long?" he demanded.

Mrs. Bolton looked up, startled.

"Did it seem like a long time?" Tanner could see her trying to transform her face into an unconcerned expression. He knew instantly that she was going to try to cover something up.

"Yes it did. What were you talking about?"

"About your headaches." She opened the door for Tanner and he felt the cold wind hit his face.

"It doesn't take half an hour to talk about headaches."

"Why didn't you tell me about them?"

"Because they're no big deal." He watched as she unlocked the car door. "You didn't answer my question. What took so long?"

Mrs. Bolton started the car and backed out of her parking stall before she replied.

"He told me that the headaches come after you have a dream about swimming."

"That's right. So? Do you think I'm crazy too?"

"Of course not, Tanner." She reached over and gave his head a friendly swat. "Dr. Thompson doesn't think you're crazy either."

"But he thinks I should see a shrink?"

Mrs. Bolton sighed. "You make it sound so terrible." She paused, thinking. "You know, everyone needs someone impartial to talk to now and again. It's completely normal."

"Name one person I know who has seen a shrink."

"Listen, Tanner. Quit calling them shrinks and I'll give you some names."

"Deal."

"Well, me for example," said Mrs. Bolton. She glanced at Tanner with a sheepish look on her face. "I saw a psychologist for awhile before you were born."

"You? Really?"

"Yes, really. Do you think I'm crazy?"

"Well … it's debatable," he answered with a laugh. He ducked, narrowly missing another swat to the head. "Maybe it's inherited. Take Nicole. She's definitely crazy!"

"So? You'll think about it?" asked his mother, suddenly serious again.

"Give me another name."

"Dad."

"Dad? Really?"

"Yep. We saw a counselor together. And it saved our marriage. Not only saved it, but taught us how to make it strong."

Seeing a counselor about your marriage and seeing a shrink about a weird dream seemed like two entirely different things to Tanner. But as he stared out the car window watching the familiar scenery go by, he realized that it would be a relief to just get it off his chest, to share the creepy dream with someone. Someone who didn't really care if he was going crazy. Someone who wouldn't make fun of him.

"Okay, okay. I'll think about it," he blurted out. "But don't say anything to anybody. Promise?"

"How about Dad?"

"Okay, Dad. But no one else. And I said I'd think about it. That isn't a yes yet. Don't go making any appointments or anything."

"It's a deal, Tanner."

.... eight

Alex stood by the railing of the ferry, looking down on the car deck where the crew was directing the last few vehicles onto the vessel. Eventually the horn blew, signaling the start of the sailing. Alex stayed on the deck and watched the activity at Duke Point for as long as he could. The lights from the homes on neighboring Gabriola Island twinkled across the water. He wondered how long it would be before he'd see this place again.

He shivered as the ferry picked up speed. Moving indoors he found a window seat and threw his duffel bag into an empty chair. The chugging of the ship's engines relaxed him and he turned to look out the window, but all he saw was his reflection in the glass. He studied his face. Brown eyes stared back at him.

"Why would I have brown eyes if both my parents are blue-eyed?" he had asked his biology teacher when they were studying genetics the year before.

"It's strange how it happens sometimes, Alex, but you must have inherited them from a grandparent, or great-grandparent. Can you think of any brown-eyed relatives?"

Alex had tried to remember one, but without success.

When he questioned his parents they told him that he had lots of brown-eyed relatives back in Poland. Funny, he thought, that only the blue-eyed ones had emigrated.

Alex blinked and looked beyond his reflection, out to the black water. His thoughts drifted back to the events of the last two nights.

After returning home from his walk with Cara on Sunday night he had found his parents still sitting around the dining room table with his relatives, drinking coffee and liqueur. Their voices were loud and Alex recognized the undercurrent of anger in his father's voice. When it sounded like that, it didn't matter what anyone said or did — he was looking for a fight. Alex decided to play it safe and stay in his room so his father wouldn't try to drag him into an argument. It worked for a while, but eventually he heard the guests getting ready to leave, so he had to put down his book to go say good-bye. He watched as they put on their coats, everyone trying to get in the final word. He wondered who was planning to drive. No one appeared sober enough, but he knew that if he said anything his father would fly into a fury. He would accuse Alex of criticizing and that was something he couldn't tolerate. So Alex bit his tongue and said nothing.

When his father had closed the door behind the last guest, he turned to Alex and, without warning, slapped his face, hard.

"Frank! What are you doing?" Alex's mother stepped between them while Alex regained his composure. He put his hand to his nose to see if it was bleeding.

"You little snot! You think you're so superior."

"I didn't say anything," replied Alex, but there was no fight in him. There was no point. He had been through it all before.

"You didn't have to. It's written all over your face. But I'm on to you, you little thief."

Alex's head jerked up. This was a new twist. He'd been

discovered. He could see from the look in his father's eyes that something was different. It wasn't just the alcohol talking this time. There was something close to rage in his father's eyes.

"That's right. I'm on to you. I've been suspicious for quite some time now, but it was confirmed when I was doing the books this afternoon. How can you steal from your own father? You're a disgrace. A no-good. I should have known you'd amount to nothing. It's probably in your genes, your blood."

Alex sighed as he stared out the ferry window into the black night. What happened next was what upset him most. His mother always came to his defense, but this time she was in the wrong place at the wrong time. When Alex ducked to avoid his father's next blow, his mother, who was beside him, got it right in the face. It didn't faze his father. Missing his target, he wound up to strike again. But the alcohol slowed him down and Alex had time to race down the hall to his room and slam the door shut.

"Let me in you miserable little traitor! I'll show you what I think of thieves."

Alex held the door shut. He hoped his father would just rant and rave for a while before giving up and collapsing into a drunken coma on his bed. That was the way it had worked in the past. The next morning he would act like nothing had happened. But this time Alex wasn't so sure. He'd finally been caught, and he didn't think his father would ever forgive him.

That's when Alex knew the time had come for him to leave. He'd hoped for a few more weeks, a chance to pay himself another hundred dollars or so, but that wasn't an option now. He had to leave that night. His only regret was not being able to say good-bye to his mother and to tell her he was sorry: sorry for stealing from the family business, sorry for being something other than the perfect son, and sorry that she had taken the blow from his father that was meant for him.

"You just wait, Alex." His father was still banging on the door. "When I get my hands on you you'll be sorry. That was going to be your station some day!"

"C'mon, Frank." Alex's mother was trying to calm the wild man down. "We can discuss it tomorrow."

"He stole from me, Pat. From you, from us." Alex could hear his father's voice beginning to calm down. Now it was a voice of despair rather than rage. He could hear them moving down the hall toward their own room, his dad moping the whole way.

"Why did he do it, Pat? Who ever heard of a person stealing from his parents?"

....

"The ferry is nearing the Tsawwassen ferry terminal. Would all foot passengers please disembark by the overhead walkway near the forward passenger lounge."

The announcer's voice brought Alex abruptly back to the present. The confrontation with his father had been two nights ago. Alex had packed a duffel bag, taken all his money and fled in the night. He had hitched a ride to Gold River and then another one into Campbell River. He slept in the bus station Monday night before catching a bus to Nanaimo on Tuesday. Now, as he traipsed toward the forward lounge, he decided to take another bus into Vancouver. It was getting late and he would need to find a place to sleep tonight. As he passed the cafeteria, he paused, smelling food. It had been a long time since he had eaten anything, but he couldn't afford to buy expensive ferry food. He would look for a late-night grocery store or a McDonald's later. He had to spend his money very carefully until he could find a job and a place to stay.

....

"How old did you say you were?" The manager of the gas station skeptically studied Alex's face.

"Eighteen."

"And where do you live?"

"At home with my parents."

"There is no address on your application. You left it blank. You also left the telephone number blank."

"We just moved. I can't remember my new address or telephone number yet." Alex was amazed at how easy it was becoming to lie. He had been given plenty of opportunity to practice during the past five days as he combed the city looking for a job.

"And you haven't listed any references. There must be someone who would be willing to give you a character reference."

This time Alex remained silent. He hadn't thought of an answer for that one even though he had heard it at least half a dozen times.

The mechanic looked at Alex sadly. "I'm sorry, Alex. You look like a nice kid but the facts just don't fit. You don't look a day older than fourteen or fifteen, and you need some references."

"Listen, I'll work a whole week for nothing." Alex was desperate. He was running out of cash and no one would hire him. "If you like my work, you can hire me. If you don't, I'm out of here. I've been pumping gas for my dad for six years and I know a lot about auto mechanics. Please give me a chance!" Alex was shocked at the sound of his own voice. He had just lowered himself to pleading, begging. But this manager looked much kinder than all the others had, and he was willing to do anything for a job.

"Then why aren't you still pumping gas for your dad? At least get a reference from him."

Alex hesitated, thinking up a new lie. "Dad and I had a

big fight. He's not even talking to me."

The manager patted Alex on the back, dismissing him. "My advice to you, son, is go apologize to your dad for whatever you did and go back to working for him." He began to walk away. Alex followed him into the station feeling more panicky than ever.

"I need this job. Please, sir. Hire me."

"I'd like to, Alex, but times are tough and I can't take the chance of hiring some young kid who could easily rip me off. I've been burnt before and I can't afford to let it happen again."

Alex turned and left. He shoved his hands deep in his pockets and began to walk down the busy city street. He thought back to how he had felt just five days ago, walking down this same street. He had been shocked by some of the people he had seen. Scary looking men, missing most of their teeth, begging for money. Kids dressed in the most outlandish clothes, gathered in groups, intimidating the pedestrians that walked by. But it was the night scene that he found most horrific. People curled up in the shelter of storefronts, wrapped in sleeping bags, spending the night on the street. Drunks, prostitutes, the homeless. He didn't think he would ever get used to it, but in five short days he had. Perhaps, he thought, because his own situation was becoming desperate, he could now understand how these people got themselves into such a fix. He shuddered and kept walking.

Overhead, the Skytrain squealed as it rounded a curve and whizzed past him on its way to the waterfront. Yesterday he had taken the elevated train to several of the communities outside of Vancouver as he went from one gas station to another, looking for work. Most of the station managers simply told him they weren't hiring, but the ones that let him fill in an application form looked skeptical when the spaces for address, telephone number and references were left blank. He didn't have a phone and if he left a phony number he'd get found out the first time they tried to contact him. He considered making up a fake address but again, it just seemed too likely that he'd get caught. All they'd have to do is phone the new listings for a Swanson family at that address and his lie would be discovered. He certainly couldn't leave the address of that seedy little hotel he was staying in. It wasn't fit for rats, let alone people. But it was cheap and better than sleeping on the street. However, he wouldn't even be able to afford that horrible little room if he didn't find a job soon.

He looked up as another train zoomed by in the opposite direction. He thought of how he had paid the fare each time he took the train on his way out of the city, but soon came to realize that it was run on the honor system. No one had checked to see if he had purchased a ticket. On the way back into the city he didn't bother. At one station an attendant did get on the train and started checking for tickets at the other end of his car. He simply got off and caught another train. He hated this lying, cheating person he was becoming, but it beat the alternative — running out of money and joining the homeless.

As he passed a pay phone he decided to try Cara's number again.

"Hello?" Alex's stomach did a somersault when he heard Cara's voice.

"Will you accept a collect call from Alex?" came the voice of the operator.

There was a pause as it dawned on Cara that this was Alex's way of contacting her.

"Yes I will." The connection instantly became clear.

"Cara, it's me. Can you talk?"

"Alex! Yeah, I'm the only one home. Are you okay?"

"Yeah. I've tried calling you but your mom or dad always picked up the phone."

"I know. They told me. But they would have accepted the charges. They're worried about you too."

"They are?"

"Yeah. The whole town is talking about you."

Alex paused. That was something he hadn't anticipated.

"What are they saying?" He smiled as he asked it. But Cara didn't answer.

"I've been so worried about you, Alex. Your mom told me about your fight with your dad. Are you okay?"

"Yeah, yeah. Don't worry. I'm okay. Haven't found a job yet, but I will. You didn't tell anyone where I was going, did you?"

"No, but they figured it out."

"How?"

"When you phoned before, the operator was able to tell my parents your location." She paused and then continued. "The Vancouver Police will be looking for you."

Alex surveyed the activity on the street around him. "That'll be like looking for a needle in a haystack."

"It's not too late to come home, Alex. Your dad will understand. He'll forgive you."

"But I'll never forgive him."

"Oh." There was a long pause. "I miss you so much. Please come home."

"It's going to work out, Cara, I promise." Alex hoped he sounded more convincing than he felt. "I'll let you know when I have a permanent address. But you can't let anyone know what it is."

"I know. I wouldn't. By the way, your dad hired Steven to pump gas."

"He did? He's already replaced me, eh?"

Cara ignored the last question. "I hear someone coming in, Alex. Will you call me again soon?"

"Yeah, I will ... And could you phone my mom and tell her I'm okay? Tell her you don't know exactly where I am, but that you did hear I was okay."

Alex hung up and flopped down on the bench in a nearby bus shelter. He blinked hard, fighting back tears. Hearing Cara's voice only reminded him of how much he missed her and his old life. Despite his dad, he liked home-cooked meals each evening and a clean bed to sleep in. The city was a loud, stinky, unfriendly place. Everything cost money, and he was quickly running out of it.

.... nine

Tanner jumped when his bedroom door flew open. Nicole stood in the doorway with a smile on her face that made Tanner nervous. He'd seen that smile before and it always spelled trouble for him.

"Hey! Ever heard of knocking?"

Ignoring him, Nicole flounced in and plunked herself on his bed. "I hear you have to go see a shrink."

Tanner swiveled around in his desk chair and glared at his sister. "Who told you that?"

"No one. I just know these things."

"I told Mom not to breathe a word to anyone — especially you!"

"Mom didn't breathe a word to me. I figured it out myself. The way I see it it's long overdue."

Tanner leapt from his chair and shoved Nicole down on his bed. He pinned both her arms behind her back and sat on her stomach. Her twisting and kicking weren't enough to throw him off and she started laughing hysterically.

"What are you laughing at?" He pulled her arms back, harder.

"Ow. What are you doing?" Despite the pain in her arms, she began to laugh again.

"I said what are you laughing at?"

"You. Owwwww! You should see your face. Owwww! Okay. Get off me and I'll tell you how I found out." Tanner began to release her arms but it only made her start laughing again. He jolted her arms back, hard.

"Owwwww!" she screamed, but something over Tanner's shoulder caught her attention and she momentarily forgot her pain. Tanner glanced back to see what Nicole was staring at. The hanging light over his desk was swinging wildly, making wider and wider arcs.

"What's going on?" Nicole asked.

Tanner didn't answer, but he released his hold on his sister and sat back to watch the lamp. It was already beginning to slow down. They both sat and stared at it until it had stopped moving.

"Was that an earthquake?" asked Nicole.

"Nothing else moved," answered Tanner thoughtfully. He was still staring at the lamp. "Beats me," he said finally. He got up and went back to his desk but swung his chair around to face his sister, who was still lying on his bed. "So what makes you think I'm going to a shrink?"

"I don't *think* you're going, I *know* you're going. I was writing something on the kitchen calendar when I noticed it said, on November 2, 'Tanner — Dr. Cunningham.' I've never heard of Dr. Cunningham so I looked him up in the yellow pages and there it was — 'Dr. Cunningham — Doctor of Psychiatry.' A shrink doctor."

"You're just too smart, Nicole." Tanner was still staring at the lamp. He'd lost interest in arguing with her.

"So why are you going?" Nicole had stopped teasing and actually sounded concerned.

"Well, it's like this. I keep having this dream. Same dream over and over. It's really getting on my nerves so Dr. Thompson thought I should talk to a professional about it. That's it. No big deal, eh?" He noticed that now it was out in the open it didn't really sound so bad after all. Everyone had weird dreams and he was just going to talk about it and see if he could make it go away. "I'd really appreciate it if you'd keep this information in the family, though, Nicole."

The swinging lamp incident had subdued Nicole, too. "Yeah, sure. I just wanted to know what was going on." With a last look at the hanging lamp, she got up off the bed and quietly left the room.

When Nicole was gone, Tanner stretched out on the bed and stared at the lamp. He cleared everything out of his mind and tried to visualize the lamp swinging. It just hung there motionless. He closed his eyes, tired from the effort. He thought about what had led up to the lamp swinging. Then he opened his eyes and stared at the lamp again, but this time he visualized Edward, his teammate. He focused on how Edward had made him feel in the locker room the other morning. He remembered the bizarre threats that Edward had directed at him. As the anger built, a knot formed in his stomach and he noticed the lamp begin to move again, ever so slightly. He continued to focus on the anger, forcing himself to feel rage, and the swinging of the lamp became more pronounced. When it was swinging wildly again, Tanner closed his eyes and forced himself to calm down. He felt his breathing slow to an even rhythm and opened his eyes. The lamp was still.

.... **ten**

As he walked past the row of pay phones in the mall, Alex slid his hand into the coin return slot of each one. Nothing. He walked through the food fair, scanning the tables for uneaten food. The mall was crazy with Christmas shoppers frantically racing from one store to the next, looking for the perfect gift. No one noticed when he quietly slipped into a chair and finished a plate of French fries and a half-eaten hot dog. A few weeks ago, eating the leftovers of strangers had repulsed him, but he was beginning to realize that you could get used to just about anything, and as one of the kids who hung out at the Skytrain station pointed out, beggars can't be choosers.

He'd learned a lot from the kids who hung out at the Skytrain station. He learned how to politely ask people disembarking from a train for their ticket stub and how to sell it, at half price, to commuters who were lined up to buy one. The commuters would check the expiry time on the stub, check their watch, and if it allowed them enough time to get to their destination, they would buy the ticket from him.

He also learned where the soup kitchens were and where

the Food Bank was located. He learned that libraries were a warm, clean place to hang out. He learned that people tended to be generous at Christmas, and a lot of money could be made panhandling outside the big hotels when the Christmas parties were breaking up for the evening. Most importantly, though, he learned how to avoid the police.

Alex had given up looking for work after three weeks of trying. Even with Christmas coming, no one was willing to take a chance on a kid with an unknown background. Finding inventive ways to supplement his rapidly diminishing savings filled his days and he forced himself not to think about what kind of person he was becoming. Although he learned their ways, Alex was careful not to become too friendly with any of the street kids. Too many of them were using the money they made to feed their drug habits.

When Christmas finally arrived, Alex spent the day in his room, miserable, hungry and depressed. He thought, briefly, of phoning Cara again, but he couldn't bear to tell her about what had become of him; how he had failed to find a job and start a new life after all. He was ashamed, knowing how worried she must be, but he didn't want her to know that he was a failure.

....

Alex stared at his hands. He noticed the dirt under his fingernails. He glanced around. No one was paying attention to him, yet. He had learned it was best not to make eye contact with anyone, so he went back to staring at his hands. He wondered, vaguely, how long he could sit here, at this McDonald's, this time, before someone asked him to move on. He had nowhere to go, though, nothing to do. The rain was pounding down. It was too miserable to go back to walking aimlessly around the streets. He had run out of options. He was tired of begging.

There was nothing to do but sit here, staring at his hands.

"You look like you just lost your best friend, kid."

Startled, Alex looked up. He hadn't noticed the woman sitting at the next table, facing him. He figured she was in her early twenties. He noticed the low-cut, snug sweater. Too much makeup, he thought, but he felt himself drawn to her. She was pretty, in a cheap sort of way, and he wondered why he hadn't noticed her perfume sooner.

"I feel like it, actually," answered Alex.

"You're a runaway, aren't you?"

"No, why do you say that?"

"Just a look I recognize."

"Well, you're wrong this time."

"What school do you go to?"

"None of your business," Alex answered, but he smiled when he said it. He felt like he was playing some kind of cat and mouse game, and she looked harmless. It was just nice talking to someone.

"Let me guess. Do you go to Vancouver High?"

"Yeah. As a matter of fact I do."

She laughed. "There is no Vancouver High. I win."

Alex laughed too. It felt good. He couldn't remember the last time he'd laughed.

"So? You gonna turn me in?"

"For sure! That's what I do for a living. As a matter of fact, I get fifty bucks for each runaway boy I turn in."

"I bet." Alex watched as she pulled a cigarette package out of her purse.

"Wanna go outside for a smoke?" She put a cigarette between her glossy red lips and searched her purse for a lighter.

"No thanks. Don't smoke."

"Don't know what you're missing."

"Right."

The woman sat tapping her cigarette on the table. Alex was aware that she was studying him, but he didn't say anything. He had gone back to staring at his hands.

"Where are you staying, kid?"

"Over on Hastings. I've got a room there." He couldn't bring himself to name the hotel.

"Some nice places over there," she replied, chuckling.

"Yeah," he answered, but this time he didn't laugh with her.

"Have you run out of money yet?"

"Not yet." He'd be damned if he was going to tell her how close he was to being broke. A couple more nights and that would be it. He wouldn't even have enough money to go back to Tahsis, defeated.

They sat in silence for a few more minutes, Alex staring into space, the woman tapping her unlit cigarette on the table.

"What's your name, kid?"

"What's it to you?" Alex didn't know why he was reluctant to tell her.

"No reason. Just tryin' to be friendly. I'm Maureen. But my good friends call me Ginny."

"I'm Ralph."

Maureen looked at him skeptically. "Funny, you don't look like a Ralph."

"You don't look like a Maureen, either."

"That's why my friends call me Ginny."

"Well, my friends still call me Ralph. But you can call me anything you want. I'm kinda between identities."

"Between identities, eh?" Maureen looked intrigued. "What was your last identity?

"Nice, small-town kid, abused by father."

"And what is your new identity going to be?"

"I'm still working on it," replied Alex. "But it's got to do with smart city kid turned independent. I'd like to be able to say rich city kid, but that seems a bit hard to achieve in this city." Alex surprised himself. He wasn't used to talking nonsense with strangers, but this game was taking his mind off his problems.

"Well, City Boy, can I buy you a burger? We're going to get charged for loitering pretty soon if we don't buy something."

"Sure." Alex felt grateful. He hadn't eaten since lunch, yesterday. He had rationed himself to one meal a day.

"What'll it be?"

"A Big Mac would be great. Thanks."

"I'll be right back."

Alex watched her as she walked over to the counter. He wondered if she was swinging her hips for his benefit or if she always walked like that. Her skirt hugged her tiny rear and her heels accentuated her long legs. No one in Tahsis looked that sexy, he thought. She suddenly turned and smiled at him, and he looked away. He knew she could read his thoughts.

She came back with a burger, large fries, large Coke and a sundae for him, and only another coffee for herself.

"Aren't you eating?" he asked, embarrassed that she had only bought lunch for him.

"I'm not hungry," she answered, still tapping her cigarette on the table.

Alex tried to eat slowly, politely, but he was incredibly hungry. As he slurped the last bit of Coke out of the cup, he looked up to find Maureen studying him again.

"You were a bit hungry."

"Just a bit. Thanks." He stretched back in his chair. With a full stomach the world didn't seem quite so nasty. He looked out the window and noticed that the rain had let up.

"So what are you going to do now?" Maureen asked.

"Do about what?"

"Your life."

Her question brought him back down from the tentative comfort zone he was floating in.

"I don't know."

"I have a friend who might be able to help you."

"Help me in what way?"

"With a place to stay, first of all. And then he could probably find you some work."

"What kind of work?"

"Don't know for sure. He was a runaway once too. Someone helped him out so now he likes to help out kids like you."

"I don't know." It seemed a little too good to be true. He knew there were people in the city who preyed on kids like him.

"What's the harm? If you don't like him, you can go back to what you are doing now," she laughed.

"True," he answered. What did he have to lose? He was too smart to get into any kind of trouble, and he had run out of ideas to help himself. "How do I meet this guy?"

"His name's Hap. I'll tell him about you. We can meet here at six o'clock tonight. I'll buy you dinner."

"Could we go somewhere else?" Alex asked sheepishly. "I've been eating here a lot lately, and I've got a craving for vegetables."

Maureen laughed. "I've never met a boy who craved veggies before. No problem. I'll meet you here but we'll go somewhere else. See you later, Ralphie, my little city boy."

She finally lit her cigarette and left the restaurant, hips swinging. As Alex watched her go he began to feel uneasy. He knew that meeting her friend was not a wise idea. But what choice did he have? He couldn't seem to get a job. It was either meet Hap or join the hungry and homeless on the street. No. He really didn't have a choice.

eleven

"Wake up, Tanner! You're having a nightmare!"

Tanner's eyes popped open. Jason's face was staring into his. Tanner bolted upright, gulping air. He felt sweat running down his back and his heart was pounding. He looked around. The other hockey players, the ones who were still awake, were watching him curiously. It was dark outside and the Greyhound bus they were riding was plowing through the night, heading west.

"You okay, man? You looked freaked!" Jason was holding a book open and the reading light from the overhead panel cast an eerie glow on his face.

"Yeah, yeah. It's like you said. Just a nightmare." Tanner leaned back in his reclining chair. The other boys lost interest in him and went back to their quiet conversations or books. "What time is it anyway?"

"It's just about midnight. You haven't been sleeping long. We've got a long way to go yet."

Tanner tried to pull himself into the present — as far away from the nightmare as possible. He knew that if he went back to sleep the dream would just continue from where it had left off. He would be back to drowning once again.

He thought back to the evening. They had played their first game of the road trip in Calgary. It had been an easy win. But it was going to be a grueling trip. It was December 27 and they had ten days of the Christmas holidays left in which to travel to the coast, play in the tournament and then get home in time for school in January. The team manager had scheduled games for the trip there and the trip back.

"You can do it, boys!" the coach had said when he handed out the trip itinerary. "You're in great shape and the extra games will give us much-needed experience. If you eat well and get plenty of rest between games, you'll have no problem. This will give you a taste of what it's like to be a pro."

Tanner had almost backed out of the trip at the last minute. The nightmares were getting worse, keeping him from sleeping. He was tired all the time and losing his appetite. But he had rested as much as possible over Christmas, and the lure of finally getting to the coast and seeing the ocean kept him from backing out. Besides, he didn't know how to tell his coach or his parents why he couldn't go. "I can't go because I have nightmares ..." sounded pretty feeble.

Tanner reached into his pack for his Tylenol.

"Whatcha doing?" asked Jason, looking up from his book.

"Just taking care of my headache."

"Again? You've got another one?"

Tanner was having trouble keeping his problems a secret. "It's no big deal." He could feel Jason staring at him. "Why don't you take a picture?" he snapped. "It lasts longer."

"You're not looking too good, man. I've been watching you. You look pale, and you got circles under your eyes. You sure you passed your physical? You don't have some kinda disease or something?"

"Well you don't look so good and you don't smell so good either!" Tanner replied, not trying to mask his irritation.

"I'm serious, man. What's your problem?"

"I'm serious too. I don't have a problem — except you. You're getting on my nerves."

"Listen, man. All those pills you keep poppin' can't be good for you. It's no wonder Coach took you off the first string. Your hockey sucks."

"Shut up, Jason."

"Shut up yourself." Jason reached up and flicked off the overhead reading light. "I'm just trying to help," he said quietly.

"I don't need your help." Tanner turned his back to Jason and kicked the wall of the bus. Why had he said that? It was a lie. He did need Jason. Jason was the only person on the team who still acknowledged that he even existed. Tanner knew that his hockey sucked. He was a wreck. He didn't even know why Mr. Jack brought him on this trip. As his hockey had deteriorated, so had his relationship with his teammates. Even Edward left him alone now that he had his spot back on the first string.

One by one the overhead lights clicked off as the boys tried to sleep. Tanner peered out the window. He knew they were in the Rockies. He could feel the bus slowing down as it scaled another long mountain pass. He pushed the button on his seat, reclining it to its furthest position. Despite himself, he thought back to the nightmare. He had been seeing Dr. Cunningham every week for almost two months, but the problem was only getting worse. Dr. Cunningham said problems often get worse before they get better. At first Tanner had hoped he was right, but he was beginning to think it was pointless, that seeing him was a waste of money. They were on the wrong track and the visits weren't doing any good. He thought back to the first session and how hopeful he had been ...

....

"Aren't I supposed to be lying on a couch or something?" Tanner asked. He looked around the office, but there was no couch to be seen. The doctor's desk was tucked into a corner and the two of them were sitting on plush chairs with a coffee table between them.

The doctor laughed. "I guess that's how it's done on TV or in books. It's not my style but if you'd be more comfortable, I'll have a couch brought in for you"

"No, no. It's okay. It's just not how I pictured a shrink's office."

"Okay, Tanner," the doctor continued. "Let's get started. Why have you come to see me?"

"Well, it's like this. I have been having this recurring dream and I always have a major headache the next day."

"Uh huh." Dr. Cunningham just looked at Tanner, waiting for him to continue.

"Well, Dr. Thompson thought that if I dealt with the dream, the headaches would go away."

"Sounds logical. What do you think?"

"I don't think anything. I just want to get rid of the dream — it gives me the creeps. And I don't like the headaches, either."

"I guess not."

"So, do you think you can help me?"

"I think I can help you understand the dream. Is that what you want me to do?"

"Yeah, I guess. I've never been to a shrink before. I don't know what to expect." Tanner wished he could tell him about the swinging lamp and the other objects that seemed to come crashing down when he was angry, but he figured that might just be enough to have him committed.

"So, tell me about the dream, Tanner."

"Well, I've had it for years, but just recently it has changed somewhat."

"Hmm."

"It always starts out as a feeling of panic — like I have to escape something. So I start swimming away from whatever it is. I am in the ocean. I'm a great swimmer even though in real life I can't swim at all. In fact, I've never been to the ocean, either."

"It's amazing what we can do in our dreams."

"Yeah."

"Do you ever reach your destination?"

"No. Sometimes I just want to float to the bottom of the ocean, but a little voice always tells me to keep going."

"And now this dream has changed?"

"Yeah. One time someone was going to hit me, so I ran. I dove into the water and swam away."

"Did you know this person?"

"In my dream I seemed to. But I couldn't tell you who it was."

"They must represent something or someone. Things in our dreams are sometimes just symbols for something else. But we'll get back to that. What else has changed?"

"Well ..." Tanner paused, trying to sort out the images that were coming to mind. "I used to feel strong when I was swimming. I felt positive that I was doing the right thing. I felt ... hopeful, I guess."

"But now?"

"Now the dreams have gotten worse — turned into night-mares actually. I get the feeling that I'm drowning — that I can't come up for air. I want to turn around and go back, but when I look back there is nothing there. I have to keep swim-ming, but there is nothing to swim toward. The waves are getting higher. I'm being sucked down." Tanner had felt his heart pounding erratically as he described the feelings to the doctor.

"Is there anything else?"

"No, that's about it. I'm almost afraid to go to sleep at night because I know the same dream is going to come back. When I'm sleeping and having the dream, it always feels like the first time, but when I wake up I realize that it's the same dream again."

"Do you have the dream every night?"

"No, but it is coming a lot more often."

"Do you have other vivid dreams, Tanner?"

"Not like this one." He wondered if he should try to explain the feeling that he was actually experiencing someone else's dream.

"Is there anything else you can tell me?" The doctor made some notes on his pad.

"Nope." Tanner decided against going into any more detail. "That's about it. What do you think it means?"

"Only you can really know what it means, Tanner. But I might be able to help you figure that out."

"Oh." Tanner was disappointed. He had hoped the doctor would know immediately what it was all about and be able to help him make the dreams stop.

"Tell me about the headaches now."

"Well, they always come in the morning after I've had the dream."

"How bad are they?"

"Real bad. My whole head pounds. I can't focus on anything when I have them."

"Do you get headaches at other times too?"

"No. Not usually."

"And now that the dreams are coming more frequently,

the headaches are coming more frequently too?"

"Yep."

"You're positive that they're related?"

"Uh huh."

"Okay. You've done the right thing, Tanner. You had a physical exam to rule out anything wrong with your physical health, so now we have to deal with your emotional health."

"Emotional health?"

"That's one name for it."

"Do you really mean mental health?"

"I guess you could call it that, but I don't think we're dealing with a disease or anything. We just have to get to the bottom of what is troubling you, so that is why I call it emotional health."

"Nothing is troubling me but these dreams." Tanner knew that wasn't quite true, but he still couldn't discuss the strange notions he had; the feeling that this was someone else's dream and the suspicion that his anger could make things move. It was best, for now, just to deal with the dreams.

"Well, I suspect you are repressing something, Tanner, and that is why you are having these dreams."

Tanner squirmed in his chair. "My life is fine except for the dreams."

"Everyone has dreams, Tanner, but to have a recurring one suggests you're not consciously dealing with something troubling you, so it comes back to haunt you at night."

Tanner knew that these weren't just simple nightmares. But how could he explain the weird things that were happening to him?

"I can see you're having trouble with this, Tanner. But you see, if you knew what was troubling you, you wouldn't be having these dreams. Hopefully by discussing it, by looking at some of the symbols in your dreams and by talking about some of the things that are going on in your life, we will be able to discover whatever it is you're repressing."

"Maybe." Tanner had hoped it would be easier than that. He had thought he could tell the doctor about his dreams and the doctor would tell him what it meant, why he was having it and then the dreams would be over.

"How long do you think it will take?"

"That all depends on how quickly we can get to the root of the problem."

"And if we don't?"

The doctor laughed. "That's not likely, Tanner. If we work at it long enough, we'll discover the problem. In fact, you might even enjoy the process, get to know yourself better."

....

Well, they had been working at it for two months now, and they weren't any closer to curing his headaches or ending his dreams. As Tanner sat in the dark, listening to the sounds of his sleeping teammates, the depression that had been slowly enveloping him over the past few weeks took hold once again. Yes, he needed help. He knew that much. But who could help him? Who would understand? If he was slowly going crazy, what would become of him? He had been looking forward to this road trip for a long time, but now he felt too tired and depressed to even care about hockey. It seemed so pointless ...

But then he thought about the ocean — how drawn to it he was. In some strange way, he felt the ocean held the solution to his problem. And he was on his way, getting closer with each revolution of the wheels of the bus. He would be there soon.

.... **twelve**

"Yo! ... Ralphie-boy. Over here!"

Alex turned in the direction of Maureen's voice. She was standing at the door of the McDonald's, cigarette in hand, beckoning to him to meet her outside. When he joined her on the sidewalk he noticed a long, white limo waiting at the curb, engine running. The windows were dark so he couldn't see inside. The driver beeped the horn and Maureen grabbed Alex's arm and pulled him into the back seat beside her. The combination of strong perfume, pungent aftershave lotion and cigarette smoke assaulted his eyes and his nose as he sat back in his seat. Two other passengers sat across from them. Maureen put her arm affectionately around his shoulder as she introduced them.

"Hap, this is Ralphie, the runaway I was telling you about. Ralphie, this is Hap and Nina."

"Hey, Ralphie. How goes it?" Hap grabbed Alex's hand and pumped it as the limo pulled out into the traffic. Nina just stared at him, her exotic black eyes glassy.

Alex reached over to the door, groping for something to

lower the windows — the combined smells were overwhelming him. Maureen mistook his movement as an attempt to escape. She pulled him closer to her, her arm still around his shoulder.

"Hey, Ralphie-boy. We haven't had dinner yet. Where are you going?"

"It's just the smoke — I wanted to roll down my window."

"Hey, my man, no problem," said Hap, and he used the master panel on the door beside him to lower the tinted glass, letting in some welcome fresh air.

They rode in silence. Alex could feel beads of sweat on his forehead. Nina was still staring at him and Hap was busy lighting another cigarette. What was he doing in this car? Where were these people taking him? He glanced up at Maureen. She smiled warmly at him.

The driver maneuvered the limo through the busy rush-hour traffic. The rain had eased up and Alex watched a ship glide under the Lions Gate Bridge as they crossed the span. The driver took the West Vancouver turnoff and headed up the hill to the exclusive homes that overlooked the city and harbor. They passed mansion after mansion before turning into a long, circular driveway.

"Aren't we going out for dinner?" Alex asked Maureen quietly as they climbed out of the car.

"We're going to have dinner here, bud. Thought you might like to eat with a view."

Following the group up to the house, Alex could hear music blaring even before Hap opened the door. He stepped into the foyer and stared at the scene before him.

The huge marble entrance opened into an enormous living room with floor-to-ceiling windows that showed off the spectacular view of the city. The blinds were open and Alex could see the steady stream of car lights crossing the same bridge that they had been on just minutes before.

The loud music was coming from the living room where groups of people were lounging about. A few looked up and waved at Hap as he came into the room, but others were oblivious to him as they sipped on drinks and blew smoke from their cigarettes. The women in the room were all young and attractive, Alex noticed. Most of the men were older and dressed casually. Hap crossed the room and turned the music off. That got everyone's attention.

"I'd like to introduce you all to Ralph, Maureen's new friend," he said. There was a chorus of hi's and Alex gave a feeble little wave in reply.

"He's here for dinner, and he'd like some veggies."

Alex's face went crimson when the crowd broke out in laughter. He wondered if he'd be able to find his way down the hill and back to the city if he walked out the door right now. But with everyone's attention focused on him, his feet felt glued to the floor.

"Come on Ralph. We're going to get to know each other over a game of pool. Nina — you go rustle up some food for the boy. Lotsa veggies — you hear?"

Nina nodded and winked at Alex. Hap led the way out of the living room and down a circular flight of stairs to the poolroom. There was a bar in the corner and Hap went straight to the fridge where he pulled out a couple of beer. He flipped off the caps and handed one to Alex.

"Thanks," he muttered and took a sip. Hap passed him a pool cue and set the balls on the table.

"You play much pool, Ralph?'

"Some."

"Good. You can break 'em."

Alex nodded, set his beer down on the bar and leaned over the table. He carefully took aim and shot the cue ball into the mass of stripes and solids.

"Nice," commented Hap. They played in silence for a few minutes. The only noise in the room was the clinking of the pool balls and the faint drone of music from upstairs.

"Where you from, kid?" Hap asked as Alex got ready to take his turn.

"The Island."

"Oh yeah. Victoria? Nanaimo?"

"No. Small town on the west coast."

"You can name the town, Ralph. I'm not about to report you to the authorities."

"Tahsis."

"Never heard of it."

"Like I said, it's small."

"Must be. What brings you to the big city?"

Alex picked up his beer and took a sip as Hap took his turn. He didn't like the taste but he felt he better drink it to show this guy that he wasn't a little kid. Besides, he needed to stall for time as he decided how much information to disclose about himself.

"I'm looking for a job. Had to get away from my father."

"Oh yeah. He rough on you?"

"Yeah, sort of." Alex took another sip of his beer. This conversation was making him uncomfortable. Hap seemed okay, but then he had ridiculed him in front of the whole room of people upstairs. He felt disorientated. He took another sip of the beer. It was beginning to taste a little better. It was also beginning to take effect, relaxing him, making him feel a little light-headed.

"Well my dad was rough on me too, but I've done okay," said Hap, motioning to the beautiful home around him.

"This is all yours?"

"You bet."

"Nice." That was the understatement of the century. Alex had never been in a ritzy home like this before. He had only seen them on TV and read about them in books.

"Any chance you gonna change your mind about being a runaway and head back home in the near future?"

"No chance. Only ..."

"Only what?" Hap looked up sharply from the shot he was about to make.

"I'd like to bring my girlfriend over someday, after I've made some money and found a place to live."

Hap looked relieved. "Girlfriend, eh? Yep. Chicks screw you up every time. You have the perfect plan, but some girl wants to change it — change you. Does this girlfriend want to come over?"

"She wants to be with me."

"How old is she?"

"Fourteen."

Hap threw his head back and laughed. "She's just a baby! Don't go and get all fixated on some baby, man."

Alex ignored him and took his turn. He sunk three balls and got ready to shoot the eight ball.

"So now that I know you're roughly fourteen and you're from some little town named Tahsis, I guess you might as well tell me your real name, kid." Hap had popped the caps off two more beer and passed one to Alex.

Alex looked up from his shot and took the offered beer. "How do you know it's not Ralph?"

"C'mon, kid. Runaways don't tell people their real names. It wouldn't be smart. But if I wanted to turn you in, I have enough information already that I don't really need your name now, do I? So let's start off this relationship by being straight with each other, okay?"

"This relationship?"

"Yeah, this relationship. I'm in the position to help you get on your feet — help you earn enough money to find a decent place to live and start a new life in the big city."

"Why would you do that for me?"

"Because I was a runaway once too. And Ginny's right — I like you. I have a good gut feeling about you. And I always have a need for young boys."

A need for young boys? Alex was just about to ask Hap what he meant when Nina came into the room with a tray of food. She set it on a low table surrounded by green leather furniture. In the corner there was a big-screen TV.

"Thanks, Nina, my love," cooed Hap. "I'll see you in a bit," was his way of dismissing her. She gave him a wink as she left the room.

"C'mon, kid, dig in." They settled themselves on the couch and Hap motioned for Alex to pick up a plate. On the tray was a steaming bowl of perogies, a platter of Bavarian smokies and a Caesar salad. There was also a large platter of raw vegetables with a dip placed in the center, and small bowls of sour cream and bacon bits for the perogies. The two beer had numbed Alex's anxiety, and he heaped his plate full. He noticed Hap only took a small portion of everything, but then, Alex thought, he hadn't been living on one meal a day for the last week.

As Alex ate, he sensed Hap studying him. When he washed down a mouthful of food with the remains of his second beer, Hap quickly went over to the bar to fetch two more. Alex ignored Hap's stares and just kept eating and drinking. When Alex finally began to slow down, Hap repeated his question.

"So what is your real name, kid?"

"Alex."

Hap stuck out his hand. "Pleased to meet you, Alex. There's nothing I like more than a kid with a good appetite."

Alex shook his hand and laughed. "That was almost as good as my mom's perogies."

"Yep. That Nina, she knows how to win a boy's heart."

Alex sat back and swilled the last of his beer. He was warm, comfortable and full. He liked the effects of the beer — it took away the edge — the discomfort of being where he was. Hap handed Alex another one and then checked his watch.

"Listen, kid. I'm heading out, so we'll have to get better acquainted tomorrow. Help yourself to as much beer as you like, feel free to watch the tube and you'll find lots of bedrooms in the hall out that door." Hap motioned to the other end of the room. "First come, first served with the rooms. I'll catch up with you in the morning."

Alex watched Hap leave the room. He flopped back in the overstuffed chair and closed his eyes. Was this all a dream? Was he really sitting in a mansion high on the hill in West Vancouver, drinking beer and playing pool with a complete stranger? What was going on? Why were these people treating him like an important guest? And what did Hap mean when he said he always had a need for young boys? He opened his eyes again. Yeah — he was here all right. But the events of the evening had taken their toll. He felt warm and comfortable for the first time in weeks. He ignored the nagging feeling that something was wrong. This was his first experience with beer and he was incredibly tired. He thought of getting up and finding a bed to sleep in, but it seemed like such an effort. He tucked his feet up under his body and lay back. He closed his eyes again. It was a mystery, all right. But it was a mystery he could live with for tonight, anyway.

....

Alex awoke with a start. He looked at his watch. He must have been sleeping for a couple of hours and now he needed to find a bathroom — fast! He got to his feet and felt the floor rise to meet him. He grabbed the side of the chair and flopped back down in it. He was so dizzy he thought he was going to throw up. He stood up again, more slowly this time and staggered out to the hall. He poked his head in the open doors until he found the bathroom — and none too soon. He could tell the party was still happening upstairs because he could hear the steady beat of the loud music through the ceiling. After flushing the toilet he splashed cold water on his face and drank two glassfuls of water. Coming out of the bathroom he noticed the winding stairs that led back up to the party. Curious, he went up a few steps, craning his head to get a peek into the living room. The smell of smoke drifted down to him — cigarette smoke combined with something different. Incense? Dope? Alex wasn't sure and didn't really want to find out. Besides, his stomach was queasy and his head was still spinning. He went back down the steps and quietly looked in the first open door. The only furniture was a double bed with a night table and lamp. The bed looked incredibly comfortable — unlike the broken-down cot he'd been sleeping on for weeks. He took off his shoes, locked the door and turned off the light. He dove into the bed and fell into a deep sleep.

.... thirteen

Tanner watched the scenery roll by as the bus neared the coast.
They had just left the scenic Coquihalla highway, where the
bus had struggled to climb some of the steep passes. It had
been snowing, and many of the cars had stopped to put chains
on in order to get through the mountains. That was only an
hour ago, but now it was practically prairie scenery again. The
main difference was that the farms were green and wet here
instead of buried under a foot of snow as they were in Alberta
at this time of year.

Tanner sat back and listened to the easy banter of the boys
around him. Their confidence was soaring because they had
won all their games so far. They were dressed in shirts and
dress pants and just had to slip into their blazers and ties to be
ready for the opening ceremonies of the tournament that
evening. Tanner wished he shared in the excitement, but he
was feeling too sick and miserable. He'd had to share a room
with a teammate each night and had forced himself to stay
awake as much as possible to avoid being caught in a nightmare again. But exhaustion wasn't his only problem. Jason

had avoided him since the fight they'd had on the first night of the trip, and Mr. Jack hadn't played him since the game in Calgary. He didn't blame the coach. His hockey had deteriorated to the point that he shouldn't be on this team. If it wasn't that he still had an overwhelming desire to see the ocean, he'd have faked illness to get sent home.

Night had fallen and it was pouring rain when the bus finally wheeled into the parking lot of the Rec Center. The boys shoved and jostled good-naturedly as they put on their jackets and ties and waited to get off the bus. Tanner stayed seated, saving his energy. He looked out the window into the gloom. There was quite a crowd milling around the entrance. There would be teams here from all over Western Canada and Washington state. They were all meeting here tonight for a banquet and the opening ceremonies, and then the games would be played at various arenas around the city for the next five days. He noticed a girl, about his age, who looked out of place. She had long, straight, brown hair and large, sensitive eyes. Tanner rubbed the moisture off the window. Man, he thought. Pretty. At that moment she looked up at the bus and Tanner could have sworn she looked right at him, although he knew the windows were tinted and she wouldn't be able to see in. He looked away and then realized how hard his heart was pounding. At least that part of me is still working, he thought. He was about to stand up and join the line of boys filing off the bus when Edward swung himself into the empty seat beside him.

"She's a babe, eh?" he said to Tanner, motioning to the girl standing outside the arena.

Tanner groaned inwardly. Edward must have been watching him gawk at the girl. The only good thing about being taken off first string was that Edward had given up trying to intimidate him. Everyone, in fact, seemed to be avoiding him now that he was having trouble with his hockey. He knew what a leper must have felt like.

"Yeah," he agreed. "I was just wondering what she'd be doing in a place like this."

"Hockey groupie, no doubt," replied Edward. "Some girls just love hockey players."

Tanner smiled to himself. "I was thinking along the lines of someone's kid sister. Anyway, let's go — it's time to get off."

Edward's glance took in the almost-empty bus. "I just wanted to have a little talk with you — make sure we got some things straight."

"Oh yeah. Like what?" Tanner could feel the familiar knot forming in his stomach. He wasn't in the mood for any of Edward's bullying.

"Now that I've got my rightful place back on first string, I intend to keep it that way."

"Yeah. So?"

Edward stood up and was looking straight down at Tanner. "So don't try any smart-ass maneuvering to get me bumped again." Tanner just shook his head and rolled his eyes.

"I'm serious — and you can quit rolling your eyes." Edward stayed put, trying to outstare Tanner. Tanner could feel the knot in his stomach growing, but he couldn't muster up the energy to fight back.

"Oh, hell. I don't know what I'm worrying about anyway," Edward said as he picked up his duffel bag and started down the aisle. "You're looking so bad I've got nothing to worry about. Wouldn't be surprised if they told me you had some kind of a disease or something."

Tanner suddenly felt the knot in his stomach give a final yank. He caught sight of the large first aid pack that was lying loose in the overhead rack above the bus driver's seat. As

Edward reached the front of the bus, Tanner saw the pack vibrate and begin to slide off its rack. He focused his attention on it, willing it to fall. Sure enough, it did, and the timing was perfect. Edward had just stepped beneath it when it toppled and fell, hitting him squarely in the back of the neck. He stumbled into the stairwell, trying to grab something for balance, but with his large duffel bag propelling him forward he tumbled right down the stairs and onto the wet pavement. People formed a circle around the prone figure, wondering who it was it and what had happened.

"Edward, are you all right?" Mr. Jack had shoved his way through the crowd and was kneeling at Edward's side. Edward pulled himself into a sitting position and rubbed the back of his neck. The coach reached out and helped him to his feet. The bus driver had rushed over and retrieved his first aid kit.

"What's this doing here?" he asked. He looked back up at the bus and saw Tanner standing at the top of the stairwell. "Are you responsible for this, boy?" he asked Tanner.

"No," Tanner replied calmly. "I was still sitting at the back of the bus when Edward was getting off. I saw it fall off the rack and hit him, though. It was the weirdest thing."

Tanner glanced at the coach and Edward who were still standing in the pouring rain, staring back at him. Their expressions were quite different. The coach was obviously angry but Edward appeared baffled and a little frightened. He alone knew that Tanner really was seated near the back of the bus as he stepped into the stairwell.

"That's the last straw, Tanner! We'll talk later." The coach turned and rejoined the crowd that was pushing to get out of the rain and into the Rec Center. The circle of onlookers had lost interest in the incident when Edward appeared unhurt. Edward was staring at Tanner, though, who was still on the bus, staring back. Tanner had never seen Edward look anything but cocky and arrogant before, so this new look of fear brought a smile to Tanner's face. He wasn't quite sure how he did it, but he knew he was back on top again, first string or not.

"Excuse me," the driver said curtly as he pushed past Tanner onto the bus with the first aid pack. Tanner moved aside politely before descending the stairs. That's when he noticed the girl again. She was still standing under the overhang of the building, but this time there was no doubt that she was staring at him — there was no window between them now. As he went down the stairs she kept staring at him, a look of shock on her face. She pushed her way through the crowd so that their paths would cross just outside the door.

"Alex!" She grabbed his arm as he approached her.

"Who?" Tanner replied.

"Alex," she repeated. "What are you doing here?"

Tanner pulled himself away from the steady stream of boys entering the Rec Center. The girl followed him, hanging onto his arm. When they were away from the mob, Tanner turned to face her.

"My name's Tanner, not Alex."

"It is?" she asked. She dropped her arm and studied him. She looked puzzled and a little upset.

"It's me, Cara," she said quietly. Tanner watched as her eyes filled with tears.

"I'm glad to meet you, Cara," Tanner replied just as softly. "But my name's Tanner and I really don't believe we've ever met. You must have me confused with someone else."

"Yeah, I guess," she replied, but she didn't take her big sad eyes off his face. "It's incredible how much you look like someone I know, but I guess there is something different about you now that I see you up close," she said.

"I wish I was Alex," said Tanner, really meaning it. Something inside of him stirred, and he didn't want the conversation to end. "Do you live in Vancouver?" he asked.

"No, I'm from the Island. I'm just here on Christmas break to visit some relatives. My cousin is playing in the tournament. My friend who looks like you is somewhere in the city and I was hoping to run into him. Kind of a stupid hope though, given how big the city is."

"Stranger things have happened," replied Tanner. He could have stood out in the rain all night talking to this girl, trying to cheer her up, maybe even take Alex-whoever-he-was's place, but he knew he was already in big enough trouble.

"I better get inside," he said. "Maybe I'll see you again."

"Maybe," she said.

....

"I don't know what to make of your behavior these past few weeks, Tanner."

The banquet was winding down and Mr. Jack had brought Tanner into an empty locker room so they could meet in private.

"I don't know what you mean," answered Tanner, without conviction.

"You know exactly what I mean," said the coach, exasperated. "Your playing sucks, you look like hell and now you're trying to get even with Edward."

"I didn't touch Edward."

"First aid packs don't just jump up and land on people who happen to be standing on bus stairs, Tanner. Give me a break."

Tanner knew better than to argue with logic.

"I don't get it, Tanner. All fall you were a cooperative kid who played well and got along with everyone. What's happened?"

Tanner just shrugged his shoulders and studied his feet.

"Are you doing drugs, Tanner? If you are you can tell me and I'll get you some help. You can trust me."

Tanner looked at him, stunned. "Get real!"

"Well, you gotta admit it, kid, all the classic signs are there. A personality change, you don't look well and your hockey stinks."

For the second time that day, Tanner felt a huge knot growing in his stomach.

"I'm not on drugs," was all he could force himself to say.

The coach sighed. "I really like you Tanner, and I hate to do this, but I'm going to have to bench you for the remainder of this tournament. That scene on the bus today was inexcusable, and you really don't look well."

Tanner was quiet. He knew how it looked, but no amount of talking would get him out of this mess.

"If you need to talk, Tanner, I'm a good listener. Hopefully we can get you back on track when we get home." The coach stood up. "And stay away from Edward. I don't want anymore trouble. You got it?"

Tanner nodded. It was all he had the energy to do.

"I'll give you a minute to pull yourself together, and then I expect you to rejoin the opening ceremony."

Tanner sat still, praying nothing would fall on the coach as he left the locker room.

.... fourteen

Alex pulled the pillow over his head and rolled away from the bright sunlight that was streaming in through the window. He couldn't remember the last time he felt so sick. His head pounded and his mouth was dry. When he tried to open his eyes to check his watch, they quickly snapped shut again. Was the sunlight always so bright?

He dozed for a few more minutes but slowly he began to remember the events of the night before — coming here and playing pool with Hap. He tried to remember if he had really polished off all that beer Hap kept passing him. He figured he must have. No wonder he felt sick. Now he knew why his father used to be so miserable on Sunday mornings.

When Alex could no longer ignore the pressure in his bladder, he forced his eyes open and stumbled to his feet. He found his way back to the bathroom, fighting dizziness and nausea. Finished, he flipped down the toilet seat and sat on it. He leaned forward and put his head between his legs. The hunger pangs he felt just yesterday were minor compared to the way he felt this morning. He looked up and noticed the shower stall across from the toilet. Maybe a cold shower would do the trick.

Feeling the cool water run down his back, Alex tried to count the weeks since he had last had a shower. In the hotel where he was staying he shared a bathroom and filthy old tub with everyone on his floor. Now he soaped weeks of dirt off his skin and shampooed his hair twice. Then he just stood in the spray, enjoying the sensation. He wished he could scrub away the sick feeling on the inside the way he could scrub away the dirt on the outside.

When he finally stepped out of the shower he realized he was going to have to put on the same old clothes he had slept in as well as worn for the last few days. But the shower had helped his hangover. He quietly made his way upstairs, not knowing who or what he would find there.

The living room was deserted but clutter from the previous night's party was scattered everywhere. There were ashtrays full of cigarette butts, and empty glasses littered the coffee tables. The smell of stale smoke disgusted him. He pushed through the swinging doors that lead to the kitchen and then stopped dead in his tracks. His whole house in Tahsis would fit into this one room. Like the living room, the kitchen was deserted and dirty dishes and leftover food covered the counters. But despite the mess, Alex was impressed by the size of it. He plunked himself into a plush chair in the sunroom that flowed off the kitchen, and stared out at the spectacular view. The twinkling lights had been fabulous the night before, but the scope of the daytime view was incredible. He studied the shape of the mountains across the water to the west and felt sure that it was Vancouver Island he was seeing. To the south and east was sprawling city as far as he could see. He picked up a pair of binoculars that were lying on the window ledge and scanned the city. He was so busy picking out familiar landmarks that he didn't hear the footsteps approaching behind him.

"Good morning, Alex," Hap said with a swat to his back.

Alex jumped. "Morning," he answered. His heart thumped in his chest. He felt like he had been caught doing something wrong.

Hap pressed a button on the coffeemaker and immediately the brown liquid began to dribble down into the pot.

"Sleep well?" he asked, reaching for a mug in the cupboard above the coffeemaker.

"Yep," answered Alex, thinking of the comatose state he had fallen into. "Thanks."

"No problem, my boy." He pulled the coffeepot out of the machine and placed his mug under the flow of coffee. "Want a cup?" he asked.

"No thanks." His stomach felt queasy. He wasn't ready to eat or drink anything.

"You ready to start work today?"

"Huh? Yeah, I guess," answered Alex, surprised by the question. "What will I be doing?"

"We'll talk about that in a bit," answered Hap as he took a big swig of coffee. "But first we'll have to spruce you up a bit." He studied Alex critically.

"Yeah, I know. I need my clothes. If someone could give me a lift over to my hotel ..."

"You're not going back there, kid. This is your home now. I hired you last night, remember?"

"But my clothes and stuff are there and I have to pay the rent I owe ..."

Hap threw his head back and laughed. Then he pulled his wallet out of his back pocket. He took out a bunch of bills and threw them on the table in front of Alex.

"Is that enough to buy you some new duds, man?"

Alex just looked at the money. There were two one hundred-dollar bills lying there plus a couple of fifties and a bunch of twenties.

"Well, yeah, but I can't take your money, and I do have to go straighten out what I owe at the hotel."

"Don't be a jerk, man. You don't owe them nothing. They'll never see you again and if my guess is right, they were hosing you anyway. They can have your crap. You're going to be a new man — from your underwear to your outerwear."

Alex tried not to show the discomfort he was feeling. Cheating on the Skytrain was one thing. Paying himself for pumping gas at his dad's gas station was something else. But not paying his rent ... he couldn't do it. He decided he would go straighten things out after he got back on his feet.

"Take it as an advance, kid," continued Hap, motioning to the money. "C'mon," he said, taking a last swig of his coffee. "We'll go get you some clothes, and then we'll go out for brunch. Then we'll talk about how you can pay me back."

Alex just nodded his head and picked the bills up off the table. How ironic, he thought, that yesterday he was practically penniless and feeling miserable, and today he had a couple hundred dollars shoved into his back pocket and he was still feeling miserable. Go figure.

....

A few hours later Alex and Hap were sitting in a restaurant drinking coffee. Alex had spent all of his advance and more. Hap had insisted on designer name fashions. He said that his employees had to look sharp. So Alex had let Hap choose a new wardrobe for him. He even had a new haircut. He wiggled his toes. These pointed boots would take a little getting used to.

While they were waiting for their pancakes, Hap made small talk. Alex was sufficiently recovered from his hangover to feel hungry again. When the food came he dug right in. He ate with such gusto that he was surprised to look up and find Hap just playing with his food. *Maybe he has a hangover too,* he thought.

"So, Alex. You feel better now?"

"Yeah. All that shopping made me hungry I guess." He wondered if it would be rude to ask Hap if he could eat his plate of pancakes, too. He hated seeing food go to waste but decided against it.

"You were looking a little green this morning."

"I was feeling a little green this morning," Alex admitted.

"Not used to drinking beer, eh?"

"No, not really."

"You'll get used to it."

Alex didn't mention that he had vowed off alcohol for life.

"So you're ready for your first job, then?"

"I guess."

"I need you to make a delivery to a locker at the airport for me."

"A delivery?"

"Yeah. Simple, eh? Think you can do it?"

"What am I delivering?" he asked.

"Just a package." Hap's eyes narrowed as he explained. "You see, you deliver the goods, I pay you and soon you'll be a free man."

A free man? Alex felt a cold chill run down his spine.

"But what are these goods? Don't I have a right to know?" Alex was tense. He didn't really want to know the answer, but the question needed to be asked. There was a long pause as Hap considered his answer.

"Listen, buddy. In my business, sometimes it's best not to ask too many questions. You do your job, I'll do mine. Get my drift?"

"Yeah." Alex avoided eye contact with Hap.

"I like you, Alex, and I don't want to see you get hurt."

"Why would I get hurt?" Alex was still staring at his hands.

"Well, it's like this, kid. You're working for me now. I didn't invest all that money in your new wardrobe for nothing. You have to pay me back."

"And after I've paid you back?" Alex spoke softly.

"Well, I think that's quite clear, Alex." There was a hint of anger in Hap's voice. "You're either working for me or you're out in the street selling that fine young body of yours. What do you think that little girlfriend back home would think of that?"

There was no answer. Alex was grinding his teeth, silently cursing himself. He should have seen where this was going. But he had acted ignorant and gone along with everything. And now he was in over his head — way over his head.

"Let's go, kid." Hap had left money on the table and was handing Alex his new leather jacket. Alex took it but didn't put it on. It suddenly felt dirty. He followed Hap out to his little red Fiat that was waiting in the parking lot.

Alex sat in stony silence all the way back to the mansion on the hill. He considered his options. There was no way he was making any so-called deliveries for Hap. Whatever was in the parcel was obviously illegal or Hap would be doing it himself. Alex wondered what it was. Guns? Drugs?

He had to disappear, but where would he go? They knew where his hotel was, and they would certainly come looking for him. He knew just enough about their operation to make them nervous, but he wasn't involved yet, so they couldn't blackmail him. He didn't have any money left. His only hope was Maureen ... perhaps she'd lend him the money he needed to disappear.

....

Back at the house the partyers from the night before were just coming to life. Bleary-eyed, they were lounging about, drinking coffee and staring at the TV

"Don't go far, man," Hap told Alex as he headed up a circular flight of stairs. "I'll be ready for you within the hour."

Alex nodded and then quickly looked around the room for Maureen. She was sitting in a corner, watching him, a little smile on her face. When they made eye contact, she winked. He jerked his head toward the stairs, indicating that he wanted her to join him downstairs. She raised her eyebrows. He jerked his head again. She gave a tiny nod but didn't move. Alex went downstairs, back to the poolroom. He found a couple of magazines on the coffee table and took them to the room he had slept in the night before. He flopped on the bed, leaving the door ajar so he could see Maureen when she came down. He turned the pages of a magazine, but his mind was elsewhere. When he saw her at the door he jumped up, pulled her into the room and shut the door behind her. His heart was pounding.

"Why didn't you tell me what kind of work I'd be doing for Hap?" he demanded.

Maureen had been smiling when she came in, but her expression changed dramatically. She pulled cigarettes out of the pocket of her housecoat and lit one before she answered.

"I didn't take you for an idiot, kid. You didn't think you'd be delivering newspapers, did you?"

"No, but ..." Alex didn't know what else to say. Maybe he had been an idiot. He had been so desperate that he wanted to believe he'd been given a chance. "Well, yeah, I guess I am an idiot. Anyway, I can't do this kind of work, and I haven't got a cent and you've got to help me."

"What do you want me to do?" she asked, eyes narrowed.

"Just lend me some money and help me get out of here."

"I can't do that."

"Why not?"

"Because if Hap found out, he'd kill me."

"He won't find out."

"He finds out everything, kid. He's got eyes everywhere. And I'm not kidding about him killing me."

"You're the only one who can help me," Alex was feeling desperate. "I'll pay you back. I promise!"

"It's not the money, kid, believe me. I like you and I'd like to help you, but it would be certain suicide for me if I did anything like that."

"This is all your fault," moaned Alex. He knew he sounded childish, but he didn't care. He felt defeated.

Maureen stubbed out her cigarette and sat down beside Alex on the bed. She put her arm around his waist and squeezed.

"It's not so bad, kid. Just do what Hap asks. He treats you fine if you just do what you're asked. He'll pay you well and before you know it you'll be on your way. I've seen lots of kids make a good start this way. It doesn't have to be a lifelong occupation."

"What would I be delivering?" Alex asked quietly.

"You don't want to know."

"Yes I do."

"It's best if you don't," she answered honestly. "That way if anything goes wrong, you're just the go-between."

Suddenly the door flew open. Hap was standing there looking furious.

"Get away from the kid," he ordered Maureen. "You know the house rules."

"We're just talking," she replied, getting up.

Without warning, Hap stepped up to Maureen and struck her hard across the face. She fell backwards, hit her head on the wall and dropped to the floor.

"Get out!" he ordered.

She put her hand up to her nose to stop the bleeding. "I'm going," she said. "Take it easy."

"What did you do that for?" asked Alex as he sat helplessly watching Maureen slide by Hap, warily watching him for any sign of another attack. He felt responsible but didn't dare say anything to her.

"She works for me, just like you do," answered Hap. "Sometimes I have to keep my employees in line." He stared at Alex, wondering if he understood the full implication.

"Are you ready to go to work now?"

"Yeah, I guess."

"Then let's go. The car's waiting."

.... fifteen

The whistle blew, jarring Tanner back to the present. The Warriors were playing their first game of the tournament. Tanner was sitting behind the glass partition separating the hockey players from the spectators. He was tired but restless. His thoughts began to float away again. He visualized the ocean. Somehow he had to get there. Being at the ocean would help him understand the nightmare that, if possible, was getting more intense than ever.

He felt someone tap his shoulder. He turned to see Cara smiling down at him.

"Isn't that your team?" she asked, motioning to the Warriors' bench.

"Yeah," he answered.

"Are you injured?"

"Sort of," he answered, grateful for an easy way out.

"That's too bad," she mumbled. She stood there quietly, looking awkward.

"Have a seat," he suggested, moving over slightly to give her room.

"Thanks."

"Is your cousin playing?" he asked, glancing at her.

"Derek's in the next game. He's down in the dressing room trying to get psyched up."

There was a long silence. Now Tanner felt awkward. He had never been good at making conversation with girls, especially pretty ones.

"What's the score?" she asked finally, to his relief.

"I don't know," he answered, and then laughed when he noticed her expression. "I was just sitting here feeling sorry for myself and not paying much attention to the game."

"Oh," she said, nodding. "You're feeling bad 'cause you can't play?"

"No, actually I'm feeling sorry for myself because I wish I was at the ocean instead of here."

"Really?" she asked.

"Yeah. I've never been to the ocean before."

"Huh," she said. "That seems weird 'cause I grew up on the coast."

They sat in silence for a few more minutes, pretending to watch the game. Tanner could faintly smell the shampoo she used, or maybe it was her soap.

"Do you want to go to the beach?" he asked, surprising even himself.

"Now?" she asked.

"Yeah." He looked toward his team's bench. "No one will miss me until dinner. How about you? Could you get away?"

"Well, I don't know," she said doubtfully. "But ... my parents let me bus around the city with Derek. I don't see what the difference would be."

"Well ..."

"Yeah. Let's do it. I'll leave a message on my aunt's machine. Then nobody can complain that I didn't tell them where I'm going."

....

A few minutes later they were standing at a bus stop.

"Where do you want to go?" she asked.

"The beach, remember?"

"Yeah, I know," she laughed. "I meant which beach."

"How should I know. Just take me to any old beach."

"Okay," she said, looking at the number on the bus that was just pulling up to the curb. "This one will do. Let's go."

Tanner plunked himself down on the seat. He felt his spirits pick up as they made their escape. He glanced at Cara and found her studying him again.

"Sorry," she mumbled, blushing.

"Thinking of your friend again?" he asked.

"Yeah ... I wish I had a picture to show you. It's unreal how much you two look alike. Last time I saw Alex, though, he was a little heavier than you and he wore his hair much longer. He talked different than you, too." She turned to look out the window, lost in thought.

Now it was Tanner's turn to study her. It was strange how they had been drawn to one another in the crowd the night before. She had a logical explanation for why she had noticed him — he looked like someone she knew. But why had he noticed her in the crowd? She was pretty, sure, but it was more than that. There were always pretty girls around to look at, but he felt an instant connection with Cara — like he already knew her somehow. Maybe Jason's theories about reincarnation weren't so ridiculous – he and Cara had known each other in a past life, had dated, had grown up and...who knows? Maybe they'd even married and grown old together. Tanner smiled just thinking about it. Their eyes met in the reflection of the bus window. She smiled back at him.

"So, who's better looking?" he teased, "Him or me?"

Cara laughed, drawn out of her reflective mood.

"You're both ugly!" she said and swatted his shoulder. "But I never could resist an ugly face."

"Thanks," said Tanner, pretending to look hurt.

They transferred twice before they finally reached the stop closest to the beach that Cara had decided on. When they climbed off the bus Tanner could smell the salty sea air. It was just as he had imagined, but more intense. He could hardly contain his excitement. He followed Cara across the street and through a playground.

"It's just on the other side of this park," she said. They began to climb a grassy slope. Knowing the ocean was within reach, Tanner raced ahead, unable to contain himself any longer. As he reached the crest of the hill he stopped dead, staring at the view before him.

"What's the matter?" Cara asked, coming up beside him and seeing the look of disappointment on his face. "The tide's way out ... just the way I like it."

"Well, it's just that I had visions of crashing waves," replied Tanner honestly.

"You don't usually find that here," Cara explained kindly. "Vancouver Island acts as a huge breakwater for this coast. You find those waves where there's open ocean, like on the west coast of Vancouver Island. But this spot has its own special beauty," she added. "Here you have this vast beach with an awesome view of the city on one side and the mountains on the other," she pointed out. "And look at all those ships in the harbor. Where else would you get a view like this? C'mon," she said, tugging on his coat. "Let's leave our shoes and socks here and walk out to the water."

"Are you nuts? It's winter!"

"Don't be a pansy," Cara answered, neatly tucking her socks into her shoes. "This isn't Alberta don't forget."

So Tanner followed Cara's lead and once he got over his initial disappointment, he began to enjoy the beach. He rolled up his jeans and waded through tidal pools that were rich with sea life. The cry of the seagulls and the sound of the lapping waves as they got closer to the water soothed the internal conflict that had been raging inside him for months. Cara watched as he squatted down to study the various shells and marine life. He picked up a piece of olive green kelp that had a hard, balloon-shaped head and a long, rope-like tail. Grasping the tail, he swung it around and around his head, finally letting it go. It flew far across the deserted beach.

"The cowboy in you comes out," commented Cara.

"No, the cowboys are from Calgary," he answered.

"What's Edmonton like?" she asked.

"Cold, flat. That's about it."

"Oh c'mon. It's a big place. There must be more to it than that."

"Well ... there's The Mall. You must have heard about it."

"Yeah ... what do you do for fun?"

"I play hockey in the winter and skateboard in the summer. Watch videos. Hang out. How 'bout you?"

"Hmm, I like crafts and reading. I jog with my mom and play computer games with my dad. We cruise the net a lot. And I hang out with my friends too."

Tanner looked down at her, sensing a sudden shift in mood again. "What is it?" he asked gently, though he suspected he already knew what she was going to say.

"I mostly hung out with Alex." Tanner noticed the tears that had sprung to her eyes. "I hope he's okay ..."

Tanner wondered what it would be like to hang out with a girl. In his group the boys and the girls hung out separately, though they were certainly conscious of each other. Glancing at Cara, he could understand why Alex chose to hang out with a girl.

Cara touched her head and looked up. "Oh no. Rain!"

Tanner had felt the first raindrop just as Cara looked up. The clouds were black and heavy looking. They both glanced back toward the park. They had come a long way.

"Let's run!" called Cara, already jogging back and pulling up her hood as she ran.

Tanner had to work to keep up with her. By the time they reached the spot where they had left their shoes, it was pouring. They scooped them up and kept on running toward the bus shelter. Tanner fell onto the bench, breathless. Cara flopped down beside him. She looked him over. "You're wet," she laughed.

"No kidding," he answered. He looked at her. "And you're dry?"

"At least I put my hood up," she said. She began to wipe the sand off her feet with her socks. Tanner watched, captivated by her efficient but gentle motions. He noticed how red her feet were from the cold. He also noticed how small and delicate they looked.

"Do you want to do mine too?" he asked, offering her his socks.

"I'd rather eat dirt," she laughed, looking down at his big muddy feet.

"That can be arranged," he said. He scraped a handful of sand off his foot and offered it to her.

"You pig!" She laughed and moved away from him. He moved closer, putting one arm around her shoulder to immobilize her, and held the mud up to her mouth. She wiggled free, laughing.

"Hurry up and put your shoes on! Here comes the bus."

Tanner turned to look down the road. As he did, Cara batted his hand that held the muddy sand. Her face lit up when she saw how the sand stuck to his wet face.

"You ..." But she didn't hear what he called her. She was up and running back toward the park. He raced after her. She was laughing so hard she couldn't keep much distance between them. He caught up and grabbed her around the waist. He pulled her down to the ground and sat on her. He felt the rain running down his back. Now that he had her pinned down, he didn't know what to with her. She was lying still, waiting for his next move. The rain was landing on her face. Her hair was getting wet — both from the grass and from the falling rain.

"You're wet," he said, and reluctantly got up. He offered her his hand and pulled her to her feet. He kept holding her hand as they walked back to the bus shelter.

"I still didn't get to the ocean," he commented.

"Yes you did," Cara answered. "We were just there."

"But I haven't put my feet in yet."

"That's true," she replied. "I guess we'll have to do this again tomorrow."

"I guess," he replied, squeezing her hand.

"Maybe we should go to Stanley Park tomorrow," she suggested.

"Whatever you think," he replied. "I'm the tourist, remember?" Then seeing the bus approach, he released her hand and quickly tugged his socks over his sandy feet. He couldn't remember the last time he had felt as excited about anything as he was about spending another day with Cara.

sixteen

Hap handed Alex a package. It was wrapped in brown paper and tied with string. It was about the size of a shoe box but very heavy. There was nothing written on it. Hap gave Alex his instructions.

"On the International Arrivals floor of the airport there is a bank of lockers on the far east wall. You're to place the package in locker number 46 and then put the key in this envelope. Take the envelope to the Dash Car Rental counter. Ask to speak to Johnny and give it to him. Don't give it to anyone else. Then get back in the car and come directly here. Any questions?"

"Nope." Alex stared at his feet.

"Repeat those instructions for me."

Alex obeyed.

"Good. Now, I need to introduce you to someone." He opened the front passenger door of a black BMW. Alex hadn't been able to see inside it because the windows were tinted black. "Alex, this is Sam. Sam will be accompanying you today. He will be watching you, just to make sure everything goes as planned."

Alex studied Sam's expressionless face. He was a huge, beefy man, with sunglasses on even though it was the end of December and the sky was overcast.

"Sam, come sit here in the back with Alex. Keep him company."

Sam heaved his heavy body out of the car and twisted himself into the back seat. Alex went around to the other side and got in. Hap leaned in the open window and patted Alex on the back.

"Now I know you'll do a good job for me, Alex. You'll see how easy it is and how all that fussing was for nothing. Get going now."

With that, the driver pulled the car out of the driveway.

Alex sat completely still. The package was on the bench between him and Sam. There was no way he was going to carry out Hap's instructions. He just had to wait for an opportunity to escape. He had to be patient. He had to keep his wits about him.

For the second time that day, Alex was driven back down the hill toward the city. The driver pulled the BMW into the lane that would take them over Lions Gate Bridge. The traffic was congested and they crept forward at a turtle's pace. Alex stared out the window, lost in thought. For the past few months he had been discouraged and depressed that he hadn't been able to find work and start a new life. But he had never considered going home. Today, however, things looked different. He knew he couldn't go through with this assignment. He was going to have to escape, and when he did Hap would come looking for him. What had Maureen said? "He has eyes everywhere." His life was in danger now. He'd had a glimpse of Hap's anger and he could only imagine what Hap would do to him. He had to leave the city. But how?

Alex watched the oncoming traffic. They were crossing the bridge now and were beginning to pick up speed. The words on a passing truck jumped out at him. Salvation Army. Perhaps the Salvation Army would find shelter for him until he could contact his parents? But would his parents take him back? Would Hap come to Tahsis looking for him? Man, he really was in a mess. But first things first, he reminded himself. He had to get out of this car.

"What the hell is going on now?" muttered the driver, laying on the horn. They had crossed the bridge but had come to a complete standstill again. The rain was pelting down and Alex peered through the flapping wipers to see what was holding them up. Ahead he could see a flagperson, directing traffic. The cars began turning off the main road onto a side road that disappeared into a forest.

"There must have been an accident up ahead," commented Sam. It was the first time he had spoken since they had left the mansion on the hill. "We're being rerouted through Stanley Park."

"Oh, man," grumbled the driver. "This will take forever." He picked up the cellular phone and began punching in numbers. "I better let Hap know there has been a delay."

Alex felt his pulse quicken as they left the main road and proceeded into the park. The forest all around them was dense. A person could quickly get lost in it ...

Sam sighed and squirmed around, trying to make himself more comfortable. He closed his eyes and hummed. He tapped out the tune with his fingers on the back of the passenger seat.

Alex tried to get his bearings. He caught a glimpse of the ocean through the trees on the right. He would have to head left, then, away from the ocean and toward the city.

They crawled along in silence for a few more minutes. The driver leaned forward and turned on the radio, probably to tune out Sam's humming. Alex waited for the right moment. Suddenly it was there. The BMW had come to a halt, held up by the traffic. Sam must have dozed off. Alex grabbed the door handle, pulled up on it and shoved the door open with his shoulder.

"Hey, whatcha doing?" hollered the driver as Alex jumped out. He ran across the road to the bank of trees on the other side. He heard Sam call his name. He glanced back and saw him heaving himself out of the car. The driver was already out, standing beside the vehicle with the cellular phone in his hand. Alex kept running. The bush was dense and it was hard to get his footing. He could hear Sam crashing through the woods behind him. Glancing back again he thought he could make out Sam's jacket through the trees. He was moving surprisingly fast for such an enormous man.

Alex kept going. He could feel branches tearing at his face and jacket. He could hear Sam right behind him.

"Stop, kid," roared Sam. "I've got a gun."

Damn, thought Alex. It had never occurred to him that Sam would be armed. But he wasn't going to stop.

"I'm serious, kid," Sam yelled. "I'll shoot."

Alex kept running. There was no turning back now.

The muffled sound of a gunshot propelled Alex forward. He tumbled out of the woods and found himself on a path. He turned right and kept running. Moments later he heard Sam's heavy footsteps on the path behind him. Sam aimed and fired again. Alex ran. He knew he'd be able to outrun Sam. He just had to keep out of his sight. The path suddenly veered right. Alex left it and crashed into the woods again. He had gained some distance on the path, and in the woods he wouldn't be such an easy target. He ran until it felt like his pounding heart would explode. He paused, leaning against a tree. He bent over, fighting to gain control of his breathing again. He couldn't hear Sam, but he wasn't sure if he had lost him or not. He pulled himself up into a nearby tree, scrambling to get high enough for a view. He sat on a branch, peering into the woods and listening for footsteps. All he could hear was the rain landing on the leaves. He waited, five minutes, ten minutes. There was no one approaching. His breathing was almost back to normal, but a feeling of nausea suddenly overwhelmed him. He managed to climb back down the tree before he began to throw up.

....

That evening, Alex sat in the office of the Salvation Army. He had found his way out of the park and had looked up their address in a phone book. The man behind the desk passed the phone to Alex.

"Call your folks, son. It's on us."

Alex dialed their number and listened to the rings. One ... two ... three ... He had no idea what he was going to say after hello ... four ... five ... six. There was no answer. After ten rings, Alex passed the phone back to the man.

"There's no one home," he said.

"I'm sorry. I know it took a lot of courage to phone them. But we'll get you a meal and a bed in a shelter for homeless men tonight. You can come back here in the morning and we'll try again."

seventeen

"Tanner! There goes your lunch!"

"Hey you dumb bird! Get lost!" Tanner swung his arms at the seagull, shooing it away but not before it had grabbed a beakful of fries from his basket of fish and chips. He had been lost in thought, watching a huge cruise ship glide into the harbor under the Lions Gate Bridge. From where he sat, on a grassy bank in Stanley Park, it didn't look like it was going to fit, but it had and was now swinging around to moor at Canada Place. He was amazed at the traffic in the harbor. The helicopters and small seaplanes that were flying in and out were somehow managing to avoid colliding with any of the smaller boats that dotted the water.

"We better eat fast. They're moving in on us." Cara motioned to the circle of gulls that surrounded their picnic table. Dozens of beady eyes watched their every move.

"Do they ever attack people?" Tanner asked nervously.

"Not that I've ever heard," she answered. "Just food."

"Well, nothing comes between me and my food," he declared. He held out a piece of fish, teasing the birds. They moved a little closer, jostling for the best position. Just when it looked like one had found the courage to snatch the tidbit, Tanner popped it in his mouth.

"You're cruel!" Cara declared. "Here you go, birds," she said and she tossed her last few fries onto the grassy bank. A wild mob dove at the scraps and a scramble broke out before the most aggressive ones eventually flew off, gulping down the food.

"And you're nuts," Tanner responded. "I would have eaten those!"

"Yeah, but you're greedy," she said as she got up to stretch her legs. "So, do you want to walk the rest of the way around the seawall or do you want to cut back through the park?"

"Which one takes longer?"

"The seawall."

"The seawall it is, then," he answered.

As they walked down the grassy slope he took her hand again. They crossed the road that circled the one thousand-acre park and joined the other walkers, cyclists and inline skaters on the seawall. A few minutes later they were standing under the Lions Gate Bridge. They paused, looking up at the amazing structure.

"So why aren't you playing hockey, Tanner?" Cara asked. "You don't seem particularly crippled."

Tanner smiled at her choice of words but wondered how to reply. He studied her face, wondering if the truth would scare her off.

"Actually, I've been benched for something I did." He began to walk along the seawall again, pulling her along.

"Really?"

"Yeah. And besides, my hockey in the last few months sucked, so I don't deserve to play anyhow."

"A slump?"

"Yeah, I guess you could call it that."

"So what did you do?"

He looked down at her. "Do you remember when our bus first pulled into the Rec Center the other night, there was a big commotion when we were unloading?"

"Yeah. Someone fell down the bus steps."

"Well, he didn't actually fall. I willed something to drop onto him and it knocked him down."

"You willed something?" She looked up at Tanner, expecting to see him laughing at his own joke.

"Yeah, I willed it," he said seriously, but in a lighter tone added, "It was your fault actually."

"My fault?" She stopped walking again and looked up at him, confused.

"Yeah," he said, smiling. "We were arguing about whether you were a hockey groupie or someone's kid sister."

"And?" she asked.

"And I didn't like his attitude," he replied, "so I willed the first aid kit to fall on his head."

"Is that something you do a lot?" she asked. Tanner could see from her expression that she was having trouble believing him.

"C'mon," he said. "Let's keep walking." He wondered how he could explain it to her. "Actually, that was the first time I ever consciously did it. But I think I've done it unconsciously before."

"Oh," was all she said.

"I noticed a few months ago that when I got really mad, things nearby seemed to move. But it wasn't until the other night that I tried to make it work for me."

"Do you think you could make something move now?"

"If I worked myself up into a rage, I probably could," he said. "But I don't want to."

"It's kinda scary, I guess," she replied.

Tanner was amazed. She believed him, he thought. She accepted his explanation, just like that. And not only did she believe him, she understood how he felt. He put both arms around her shoulders and hugged her hard, fighting back tears. After a moment, though, he noticed she wasn't hugging him back, so he loosened his squeeze.

"Sorry," he said, looking down at her, "I was just so relieved to share that with someone. C'mon. Let's keep going."

This time it was Cara who reached for his hand. She squeezed it when he glanced at her, puzzled. They walked in silence for a few minutes, both lost in thought.

"So, I guess Alex was your boyfriend, eh?" Tanner swallowed hard. "Or is your boyfriend?" he added.

"Is, I guess," she answered. "And, yeah, I feel a little guilty about being here with you. But he ran away from home and I haven't heard from him for a while. I don't know what's going to happen because he doesn't plan to come back to Tahsis and I don't plan to leave — not in the near future anyway."

The words "ran away" struck a chord in Tanner's mind, but he put it aside.

"Are you just here with me because I look like him?" he asked.

Cara gave a nervous little laugh before she answered. "Well, I guess that's why I first noticed you, but aside from your looks, you're not anything like him."

"You didn't really answer my question," he pointed out.

"No, I guess I didn't," she said. "This is Second Beach we're coming up to. Do you want to sit on those logs for a while?"

"Yeah, if you promise to answer my question," he said.

"Yeah, okay," she laughed, searching for a log that was reasonably flat on top. When they were seated she said, "I don't know why I'm here with you. Until two days ago I was planning to wait for Alex forever. But I've been really ... drawn to you is the only word I can think of. And besides, you'll be going back to Edmonton in a few days so this won't really matter anyway."

There was a long silence. The weather had completely changed and Tanner watched the sunlight sparkle on the water. Then he glanced back at the stream of cars driving past on the road behind them. Looking around, he noticed he and Cara were the only ones on the beach.

"It matters to me," he said, finally.

Cara sighed. "Yeah, it matters to me too."

Those were the words Tanner had been waiting to hear. Slipping his arm around her shoulders, he pulled her closer to him. Then he reached over and turned her face to his. Ignoring the look of uncertainty in her eyes, he leaned forward and kissed her gently. She didn't push him away so he kissed her again, a little more intensely this time. He felt her respond by running her fingers up his back and returning his kiss, tentatively at first, but with increasing passion ...

Suddenly there were strong hands gripping his shoulders, yanking him away from her.

"Let's go, lover boy. The game is up."

"Let go of me," said Tanner, squirming to free himself from the tight hold of the huge stranger. But the man hauled him off toward the road. Cara ran behind, pulling on the stranger's arms in an attempt to free Tanner, but with one swift kick the man knocked her away. She lay sprawled on the ground, struggling for breath.

"What are you doing?" demanded Tanner. "Let me go."

"Nice try, kid. That's the last time you'll ever get away from me. I underestimated you." They had reached the road, and Tanner saw the black BMW idling at the curb, apparently waiting for them. He was shoved into the back and then the stranger climbed in beside him. The car pulled away and joined the flow of traffic moving through the park. From where she was lying on the pavement, Cara strained to read the license plate number, but it was just out of view. She watched helplessly as the car disappeared from sight.

.... eighteen

Alex squinted into the sunlight as he pushed open the door of the shelter where he had spent the night. He couldn't believe the change in the weather. The usually rainy December skies had cleared and the sun felt warm on his head and shoulders. From this vantage point he had a spectacular view of the snow-capped North Shore mountains and he could identify the chairlifts of three separate ski hills. It was an amazing city. He wished he could stay.

He hustled straight to the Salvation Army. He didn't want to be on the street in the open any longer than he had to be. Arriving safely, he found that the clerk he had spoken to the night before was still there.

"I'm glad to see you back, son. I was afraid you'd lose the courage to tackle that phone call again."

Alex grunted. "I haven't got a choice."

"Everyone has a choice. But making the right one is not always easy. Sometimes we have to swallow our pride."

"Tell me about it."

"Well, here's the phone. Take your time. I'll be down the

hall if you need me." With that, the clerk pushed back his chair and left through the door behind him. Alex sighed and picked up the receiver. Slowly, he dialed the number. He heard it ring once, twice, three times. He was losing his nerve. What if his father answered? What would he say then? He considered hanging up.

"Hello?" Phew, he thought. It was his mother, not his father, but her voice sounded dull and flat.

"Mom. It's me."

"Alex?" Now he could hear doubt in her voice, mixed with a trace of hope.

"How many other sons do you have?"

"Oh, Alex. I can't believe it. Are you okay?" She started to laugh but the laughter quickly turned to great heaving sobs.

"Yeah. I'm fine. Don't cry, Mom. It's okay."

"Where are you?" she asked between sobs.

"Vancouver."

"Oh, honey, I've been so worried." Alex noticed she used the I instead of we, but decided to ignore it.

"I didn't want to hurt you, Mom, but I had to leave."

"I know. I know. Oh, Alex, it's so good to hear your voice." She began to sob so hard that Alex became concerned.

"Are you okay, Mom?"

"I will be now that I know you're okay." Alex could hear her blow her nose and clear her throat, trying to gain control of herself again.

"Where's Dad?"

There was a long pause before she answered. "Your dad's moved out."

"He's what?"

"He's just over at the motel."

"What's going on?"

Mrs. Swanson sighed before she answered. "After you left,

Alex, he was always in a rage." Alex could hear his mother's voice tremble. He could only imagine what his father did with his rage.

"So how did you get rid of him?"

"I called the police."

"You're kidding!" Alex couldn't imagine his mom having the nerve to get anyone else involved in their problems.

"Anyway, honey, don't worry about me. I'm just so relieved to hear your voice. Are you coming home?"

Alex realized that going home was not what he thought it was going to be. His parents' separation took him completely by surprise, and he needed time to think about the implications. Then he remembered that Hap would probably go to Tahsis looking for him. "I can't, Mom. I'm in some trouble."

"What kind of trouble, honey?" she sounded worried, but not angry like his father would have been.

"Well, it's a long story, and I promise to tell you what happened, but it wouldn't be safe for me to come home."

"Oh." She paused, thinking. "Do you want me to come there?"

"Would you?" Alex realized that he hadn't known what kind of help he was going to ask for. But if his mom would come to Vancouver, without his dad ...

"Actually, Alex, that would suit me perfectly. I've been wanting to get out of Tahsis, but I felt I had to stay in case you ..."

Alex felt sick realizing the ordeal he had put his mother through. She probably wanted to put as much distance between herself and his dad as possible, but because of him she hadn't been able to leave.

"How soon can you get here, Mom?" Alex realized he sounded like a little kid, but he couldn't help it. He felt like one.

"Well ... listen. I'm going to call John and see if he can put us up for a while." John was his mother's older brother who lived in a suburb of Vancouver. Alex didn't know his mom's family very well — thanks to his dad who always insisted on spending every holiday with his family — but from what he could remember, his Uncle John was a kind, though odd, little man. He vaguely remembered his home from a visit they had made there many years ago when they had come to the Vancouver airport to pick up some visiting relatives. It was comfortable, and as a small boy Alex had been impressed by the loud roar of the airplanes as they prepared for landing at the nearby airport.

"Will you get here by tonight?"

"I don't know, but I'll try."

Alex considered his situation. He knew he was in danger of being captured by Hap again.

"Mom. Could you ask Uncle John if I could go there tonight even if you don't make it?"

"Of course, Alex." She sounded surprised. "I'm sure he'll say yes. Why don't I give you his number, and you can phone him in about ten minutes after I make the arrangements."

"That would be perfect, Mom."

"I can't wait to see you, honey."

"Me too, Mom. And Mom ..."

"What is it, Alex?" There was that worried voice again.

"I'm sorry ... about everything."

"Me too," she sighed. "But it's going to be okay ... I just know it."

"Oh, Mom?"

"Yes?"

"Could you bring me some clothes?"

....

His uncle picked up the phone after the second ring.

"John here."

"Uncle John, it's Alex, Pat's son."

"Ahh, Alex. Your mother said you'd be calling. All the arrangements have been made. You're to come here tonight, and your mom will join us as soon as she can. I'm so glad she called, but so sorry to hear that things are not going too well."

Alex wondered how much his uncle knew.

"I really appreciate this, Uncle John. There's just one thing. How do I get to your place?"

"Where are you coming from, Alex?"

"The Salvation Army, downtown Vancouver."

"The Salvation Army. Oh." Alex's uncle paused. "How do you plan to get here, son?"

"I haven't figured that out yet."

"Well I'll come and get you then. I'll be there in thirty minutes. I'll be driving a Ford Taurus."

"Thanks, Uncle John. I really appreciate it."

....

Alex spent the next half hour pacing in the office of the Salvation Army. The clerk had come back into the room and had brought Alex a Coke and a donut. Alex didn't dare wait on the street. There was too much risk of being spotted by Hap. Alex took Maureen's earlier warning to heart and stayed as far back in the office as he could until he saw a gray Ford Taurus drive slowly down the block. How could he tell if it was his uncle or one of Hap's men, he wondered.

"I think that's my ride," he said to the clerk who was back at his desk. "I'm going to go check it out. If I don't wave to you before I climb into the car, call the police."

The clerk frowned, but nodded. "I'll come with you," he said.

Alex gratefully accepted this offer, and they waited on the sidewalk together. A minute later Alex could see the small gray car approaching them again after making a trip around the block. It pulled up to the curb. The driver leaned over the passenger seat and pushed the door open.

"Alex?" he asked. Alex recognized the elf-like face that was so much like his mother's.

"Yeah, hi Uncle John." He turned and shook the hand of the clerk from the Salvation Army. "Thanks for everything," he said. "I'm going to be okay now." The clerk squeezed his hand and watched as Alex climbed into the passenger seat.

"No bags?" asked his uncle.

"Nope. Just me."

"Then we're off." He swung the car back out into the traffic and Alex waved at the clerk who watched them drive away.

They drove along in silence. Alex was relieved that his uncle wasn't one for small talk or one to pry into Alex's situation.

"You're not working right now?" Alex finally asked.

"Nope. I retired a few years back."

"Oh." Alex was embarrassed that he didn't know anything about his uncle. Why hadn't his mother insisted on staying connected with her family over the years? He was just beginning to understand the control his father had over his mother's life.

"I'm not used to having people in the house, Alex, but let me assure you, I am very happy to have you and your mother stay with me for as long as you need to."

"We really appreciate it, Uncle John." It sounded limp, but he didn't know what else to say.

"Your mother and I were very close when we were growing up, and it has always distressed me that we haven't stayed in touch over the years."

"Hmm."

"Now, you need to tell me what you like to eat so I can

provide it. I haven't had teenage boys in the house for quite some time."

Alex wondered what had become of his cousins, Uncle John's two grown sons. It was quite a few years ago that his Aunt Theresa, John's wife, had died of cancer.

"Believe me, Uncle John, after what I've been eating for the last two months, anything will taste good. Anything but McDonald's, that is."

....

That evening, Alex's mother phoned to say that the road was closed between Tahsis and Gold River because of flooding, so she would be another day or two arriving. She was looking into hiring a seaplane. Disappointed, Alex sat with his uncle in the den watching TV.

"That kid looked like you!" exclaimed his uncle suddenly.

Alex sat up. He must have dozed off. "What kid?"

His uncle was staring at him, looking troubled. "On the news they just showed the picture of a kid who was abducted in Stanley Park today."

"Really? Stanley Park?" Was it just yesterday that he was being shot at in Stanley Park?

"Yeah." His uncle was staring at the TV again. "They said he was visiting Vancouver from Edmonton. He was with a hockey team. What a shame."

"Well, as you can see it wasn't me," said Alex, stretching. "I'm here, in the flesh, and you certainly didn't abduct me." He yawned and stretched. "But I'm beat. I think I'll hit the sack."

"Yeah, me too," said his uncle, but he still looked troubled. "Have a good sleep, Alex."

"Thanks. You too."

But Alex didn't. He lay awake for a long time wondering

about the boy who had been abducted in the park. His uncle's words haunted him. "That kid looked like you!" There was no doubt in his mind that Hap would have been scouring Stanley Park hunting for him. Hap knew that he had no money and nowhere to go. Had they abducted the wrong boy — someone who looked like him?

....

No! No! Stop! AHHHHHHHHHH! Please stop!

Alex awoke with a start. He was drenched in sweat. He turned on the bedside reading light and sat up, trying to calm his breathing that was coming in ragged puffs.

Man, he thought. That was some nightmare. When he had finally calmed down, he lay back down and turned off the lamp. But this time the screaming was back in his head before he had even closed his eyes. He bolted upright and grabbed his head with both hands. The screaming was intense. Someone's voice was in his head and it was in terrible pain. He rocked back and forth, holding his head and willing the voice to go away. But it didn't. He wondered if he was going crazy. It was horrible. He became desperate. If he couldn't will it away, maybe he could talk to it.

"Who are you?" he said to himself. "I feel your pain. What's going on?"

There was a momentary pause in the screaming. Had the voice heard him? But then it resumed, as insistent as before.

Slowly the screaming gave way to moaning, and Alex tried to reason with it again.

"What's wrong? I want to help you," he said to himself as forcefully as he could. But the voice didn't answer. It just continued to moan softly, and then it was gone.

In the morning, Alex found his uncle at the kitchen table, staring at the morning newspaper. He looked up when Alex came into the kitchen. He looked troubled, just as he had the night before. Alex wondered if he always looked like that.

"Morning, Uncle John."

"Uh, yeah, morning, Alex."

"Is everything okay?"

"Well, yeah, it's just that ..." he gestured toward the newspaper, seemingly unable to speak further.

Alex walked around behind him and peered over his shoulder. There, staring back at him from the table, was a picture of himself. The headlines stated: *Edmonton Youth Snatched From Stanley Park*.

.... nineteen

Hap was also staring at the morning newspaper. After reading the front page he grabbed the whole paper and headed up the circular stairs. He pulled some keys out of his pocket and unlocked one of the doors in the long hallway.

"What was that crap about you being a runaway from Tahsis?" he roared as he barged in. Tanner lay on the bed. He tried to open his eyes but only succeeded in opening one. The other was swollen shut from the repeated kicks to the face he had received the night before.

"I told you," Tanner tried to say, but his lips were cut and swollen like his eyes. "You've got the wrong person. I don't know what you're talking about."

Hap shoved the newspaper in front of Tanner's face. "Is this you?"

Tanner tried to focus his blurry vision on the picture. "Yeah," he grunted.

"It says here you're with a hockey team from Edmonton."

"I am!"

"You told me you were from the Island. That you were a

runaway!"

"No I didn't!

"Liar! What kind of a game are you trying to play with me?"

"I'm not," insisted Tanner, but even with his blurred vision he could see the look of disbelief on his captor's face. He wondered if the man was crazy.

Hap stared at Tanner, his eyes wild. No punk had ever messed with him before. His *staff* usually let the new boys in on his reputation. "Do you know who you're dealing with, kid?"

"No."

"You're dealing with me!" Hap wound up and smacked Tanner across the face. Tanner groaned and slumped to the floor. Hap began kicking him again, over and over.

"No one plays games with me. You hear? Never! No one! You're going to pay for this." He kept on kicking Tanner, even after Tanner had slipped into unconsciousness again.

"You're going to wish you were never born," he whispered to the limp body just before he left the room.

twenty

Alex continued to stare at the picture in the newspaper as his uncle cracked some eggs for their breakfast. This boy didn't just look like him. This was a picture of him. He had read the article twice in case he had missed something that would help him understand what was going on. The article said that the boy's name was Tanner Bolton and that he was visiting Vancouver from Edmonton with his hockey team. He had been sightseeing in Stanley Park with a friend when he was abducted.

No wonder his uncle was troubled by this picture, thought Alex. But what his uncle couldn't know was that it was him, Alex, that was supposed to be taken — not someone who looked just like him.

Alex and his uncle ate in silence. A throbbing pain had taken hold of Alex's head. Suddenly he knew what he had to do. He was the only person who knew where this boy was, and he was the only person who could lead the police to him before Hap killed him, if he hadn't already. His Uncle John must have been working something out in his mind, too, because they both spoke at once.

"Alex ... "

"Uncle John ... "

They both paused, waiting for the other to continue, but after a moment, Alex jumped in. "There's something I have to do today. Could you drive me to the Vancouver Police station?"

"Sure," replied his uncle, looking surprised.

"Was there something you wanted to say?" asked Alex.

"No, no, I guess not."

Alex knew his uncle was studying him as he put his dishes in the sink and got ready to go out. He still looked like he wanted to say something but was holding back. Maybe he was just worried about me, Alex thought.

Alex was wearing the same clothes for the third day in a row, the clothes that Hap had bought. He pushed his arm into the sleeve of the new leather jacket. He detested wearing it but he had no choice until his mother brought him some more clothes.

Less than an hour later, Alex's uncle pulled his car up outside the police station.

"Do you want me to come with you, son?"

"No thanks. I have to do this alone."

"Call me when you're ready to come home."

Home. Alex liked the sound of that word. "I will, thanks."

Alex walked bravely into the police station. The clerk at the reception desk stared at him for a moment before jumping up.

"Aren't you the kid ..."

"No. I just look like him. But I have some information that may help you find him."

The police officer had come around from behind the counter and now indicated for Alex to follow him down a long corridor. He took Alex into an empty room and asked him to wait there. A moment later he was back with three other police officers.

Everyone was silent, just staring at him. Finally, one of them broke the ice.

"You say you're not Tanner Bolton, the boy who was abducted from Stanley Park yesterday?"

"No. But I saw his picture in the paper. I know I look like him. And I think the abductors may have thought they were taking me."

"Well, I can see how there would be some confusion," the officer continued. "What is your name?"

"Alex Swanson. And I'm from Tahsis, on the Island."

"And you don't know Tanner Bolton?"

"Nope."

"Okay, Alex. We need to get your story, then. Do you mind if I tape it?"

"No. But I'm really worried that this Tanner is in a lot of danger. In fact, I'm quite sure he is, and I think I can help you find him."

Alex looked around the room at the faces. They were all looking puzzled and unsure, as if they didn't believe him. One of the officers had left the room and came back with a tape recorder.

"We have to use proper police procedure, Alex. But we'll work as fast as we can. You can understand that we can't send men out on a wild goose chase."

The tape recorder was set up in front of Alex.

"Tell us your story, son, giving us as much detail as you can."

So Alex explained how he had run away from home back in October and how desperate he was when he met Maureen. He told about being taken to Hap's house, how he was supposed to deliver the package to the airport and how he had escaped in Stanley Park.

"Which day did you jump out of the BMW?"

"Day before yesterday."

"And where have you been since then?"

"I went to the Salvation Army for help and they found me a shelter to sleep in that night. The next day I phoned home and my mom put me in touch with my uncle in Richmond. I spent last night there."

"And that's where you saw the picture in the paper and decided to come and talk to us."

"Right."

"Why didn't you come directly to us after you escaped in Stanley Park?"

"You don't understand how powerful Hap is. I was sure he'd have one of his men planted outside the police station just waiting to nab me before I could even get in. I was just thinking of saving my own neck, I guess."

"Well, that's a good plan, son," said the officer, kindly. "We can't fault you for that. Now, you say you can lead us to this Hap fellow's house?" he asked as he clicked off the tape recorder.

twenty-one

Hap lit another cigarette as he paced around the empty kitchen. He couldn't believe the boy hadn't confessed and spilled his guts before the second beating. He had never met anyone with so much stamina.

He took a long pull on the cigarette. He'd read the boy wrong, he thought. What an acting job the kid had pulled off. That hard luck story about being a runaway from an abusive home had been so convincing. But the newspaper report set the record straight. The boy was from Edmonton, part of a hockey team. And now he seemed to have forgotten all about his story of running away from Tahsis. What was he trying to prove?

Hap threw the cigarette into the sink where it sizzled out. He stared out the window, looking down the hill and across the harbor to Stanley Park. Sam had snatched the boy from the park yesterday. Sam knew who he was after, didn't he? When they had brought the kid back to the house, Hap had ordered that he be taken to the upstairs bedroom. He had gone in there then and had started roughing the boy up without taking a good look at him. But why wasn't this kid wearing the leather jacket Hap had just bought him? Where did he get the change of clothes from? And why had he been hanging around out in the open where he could be spotted. He must have known they'd come after him.

Did they have the wrong boy?

"Damn!" Hap kicked open the swinging door that led into the living room.

"Maureen, get in here, now!" he hollered at the group huddled around the coffee table. They were staring at the newspaper that featured Alex's picture and were quietly discussing the story. The scene last night had made everyone nervous. No one made eye contact with Hap, not even Maureen as she walked past him into the kitchen.

Hap lit another cigarette and threw the package across the table at Maureen. She picked it up and pulled one out. Hap leaned forward with his lighter and held a flame steady for her.

"I'm wondering if I have the wrong boy," he said, eyes narrowed, voice tight.

"Can't you tell by looking at him?"

"Not anymore. His face is swollen up like a balloon."

"Yeah, but Sam knew him. Must have known whether it was Alex or not."

"Yeah, well, maybe Sam's vision's not so good. The facts aren't jibing. Why wasn't he hiding from us? Where did he get the clothes? Who was the girl he was with?"

"Shouldn't you have thought about that before you ... you know, roughed him up, as you say?"

"Hey, I assume everyone does their job right, including Sam."

"So, what do you want me to do?"

"Go talk to him. Do what it takes. Figure out if it's him."

Maureen sighed. "And if it is him?"

"None of your business. You should have kept your feelings out of it in the first place. A girl like you should know better!"

"He's just a kid, Hap. Give him a break."

Without warning, Hap flung out his arm and smacked Maureen across the face with the back of his hand.

"Just do what you're told, Maureen. You know the game."

....

Maureen let herself into the room quietly. She had brought a bowl of water, a washcloth, a towel and some first aid ointment with her. She looked at the body lying on the bed. No wonder Hap couldn't tell who it was, she thought. His face was beyond recognition. She sat on the edge of the bed and ran her hands through his hair gently, like a mother waking her child from a nap.

"Hey, Alex, it's me, Maureen."

There was a small groan from the inert body.

"I've come to clean you up a bit, to see if I can make you feel a little better." As she continued to run her hands through his hair, she assessed the prone figure. The hair color was the same, as was the cut. He seemed to be about the same height and weight as she remembered, too.

"Hey, Alex, you remember me?" Maureen thought she could see the faintest shaking of the head. She dipped the washcloth into the warm water and began to clean some of the dry blood off the side of his face. She hummed quietly while she worked. She managed to get him to roll over so she could do the other side of the face. When she was finished, she undid some of the buttons of his shirt so she could see the damage done to his body. Oh man, she thought. Hap's an animal. There wasn't an inch of body that wasn't covered in bruising, but there didn't appear to be any open wounds so she did the buttons up again.

"I'm going to the kitchen to get a couple ice packs for you, Alex. When I get back, we'll talk. Okay?"

There was a barely visible nod.

"I'll nuke some soup for you too, okay?"

Another faint nod.

....

Hap was waiting in the kitchen.

"Well?"

"I don't know yet. The body looks like him, but I haven't got him to talk yet. I just came down for an ice pack and some soup."

"Well, hurry it up. I got to figure out what to do with him, and I can't figure it out until I know who we're dealing with."

"Okay, okay." She stood beside the microwave, waiting for the soup to heat. She lit a cigarette.

"What are your choices?"

"None of your business," he answered, then sneered, "and besides, I wouldn't tell you. You've become too soft and mushy."

The microwave beeped, and Maureen stubbed out her cigarette. She put the bowl of soup and the ice pack on a tray and started back up the stairs. She wondered, uneasily, if she could protect this boy, whoever he was, from Hap. She stopped in the bathroom and got some Tylenol out of the medicine cabinet. When she entered the room she could see he had tried to open his eyes, as much as they would open anyway, and was watching her approach. She pushed the fear she felt for him out of her mind and gave him a big smile.

"I'm back, just like I promised," she said. She put the tray on the side table and sat down beside him on the bed. "Now, let's see if I can help you sit up." She put one arm under his shoulder and steered his arm around her waist. "Okay, easy now, one ... two ... three ... up."

With a groan, Tanner allowed Maureen to pull him into a sitting position. He was throbbing everywhere and felt dizzy as he sat up.

"I'll keep my arm around you until you're feeling steady," she offered, noticing the effort it took to stay upright.

"Are you a nurse?" he asked. He couldn't move his lips, but his tongue was still working and the question came out in a sort of growl.

"A nurse?" she asked laughing. "You're joking, right, Alex?"

When he shrugged his shoulders, Maureen realized that it wasn't a joke. He didn't recognize her.

"How 'bout if I feed you this soup. Then when you get some strength back we'll put the ice packs on the worst injuries. Okay with you?"

Tanner nodded. He could smell the soup, and despite the pain he did feel hungry, or at least a little thirsty.

Maureen ladled one spoonful at a time up to Tanner's lips. Because they were so puffy and sore, much of the soup just ran down his chin, but enough made it in that he was able to feel some of his strength return. He swallowed two capsules of Tylenol with a spoonful of soup.

"There," she said, when the soup was finished. "Now I'll puff up these pillows, and we'll make you comfortable." She propped the pillows at the head of the bed and then helped Tanner swing his legs back up onto the bed and rest himself against them. She laid a blanket over him and handed him an icepack for the most damaged eye.

"Is that a little better?" she asked, sitting down beside him.

He nodded but didn't try to speak. She could see him studying her through the little slits that were all that was left of his eyes.

"So why did you run, Alex? I told you that you'd be okay if you just did what Hap told you to do. It didn't have to end like this."

"I'm not Alex," came the growled reply.

"You don't have to play that game with me," Maureen responded softly.

"There's no game. I'm not Alex." This time the words were spoken a little more forcefully.

Maureen studied him. He was a mess, but despite the disfigurement that kept her from seeing him clearly, Maureen believed him. This was not the kid she had met a few days ago at McDonald's. Hap had the wrong boy. And this time he had gone too far.

"Who are you?" she asked softly.

"Tanner Bolton."

"Listen, Tanner. There's been a horrible mistake. But I'm going to do everything in my power to get you out of here safely, okay?"

Tanner nodded and closed his eyes. The Tylenol was working and he could feel the wonderful comfort of sleep descending on him.

....

Maureen found Hap still staring out the window toward the city.

"You've got the wrong kid."

Hap swung around. "You sure?"

"Positive."

He studied her. "You're just saying that to protect your little boy."

"You asked me to find out. I found out. That boy is telling the truth. He is Tanner Bolton, from Edmonton."

"Damn!"

"So now what are you going to do?"

Hap began to pace again. "Alex could be leading the police here right now, as we speak. We have to get that boy out of here, immediately."

"What are you going to do with him?"

"He's Sam's problem now. He knows how to take care of pests. Go find him and tell him to get going."

....

Maureen found Sam in the poolroom, sitting in a corner watching a talk show on the big-screen TV.

"Sam. Hap says you're to take that boy to a secluded bushy area and leave him — alive. You've got the wrong boy and he doesn't want anymore trouble. And you're to go now."

"Alive?"

"That's what he said."

Sam heaved himself out of the chair and thundered up the stairs. He'd heard the rumors that he had snatched the wrong boy, and it made sense. The boy they abducted had acted very strangely, as if he really didn't know why they were chauffeuring him back to Hap's. Well, he wouldn't blow it this time. He'd get that boy out of here, fast. And he knew just the place to dump him. He scooped the unconscious boy up in his beefy arms, flung him over his shoulder and hustled back down the stairs. Hap met him at the door.

"You know what to do, Sam?"

"Yep. I won't screw up this time, Boss."

"I know you won't Sam. This is what you're good at."

Sam gave Hap a puzzled look and was just about to clarify what it was he was supposed to do with the boy, but Hap was anxious.

"Hurry, man, hurry," he said as he shoved him out the door and into the waiting car. Tanner was thrust into the back seat, barely conscious. Sam turned the key in the ignition and backed out of the driveway. Hap waved, relieved to get him out of the house.

Maureen watched the car from an upstairs window. Knowing she had probably just saved Tanner's life eased the guilt she was feeling for getting Alex mixed up with these people in the first place. Now she would be leaving too. She'd had enough. She just had to wait for her opportunity.

twenty-two

Alex closed his eyes and rubbed his temples. The headache was excruciating.

"Are you sure it was the Lions Gate Bridge, son?" asked Constable Russell, the police officer in the passenger seat. "There's a lot of bridges in this city."

Alex was in the back seat of the police cruiser that was making its way toward the bridge. "Yeah, through Stanley Park." He had opened his eyes to answer. "Then take the West Vancouver exit."

It had taken two hours for the police to do the paperwork needed to obtain the search warrant. They'd had to contact the West Vancouver Police force to coordinate the operation. It was agreed that the Vancouver Police would do the search because they had Alex to direct them to Hap's home. The West Vancouver Police would be on standby for backup should it become necessary.

Alex had paced the lobby the whole time. He had urged the officers to hurry, but it hadn't helped. Now they had reached the bridge only to come to a dead stop because of the traffic.

"Can't you put on the sirens or lights or something to get us through this tie-up?"

"I'm afraid not, son. You'll just have to sit tight."

Alex did his best, but the throbbing in his head coupled with the pounding in his chest nearly forced him to jump out of the car and run across the bridge. Eventually their car reached the crest of the span and began to pick up speed on the downward slope. Once again Alex watched the activity in the harbor on either side of the bridge. Was it only three days ago that he had crossed this bridge in Hap's limo? It felt like a whole lifetime ago.

As the police cruiser headed up the hill toward the exclusive West Vancouver homes, Alex's anxiety took on another dimension.

"You've got to promise me that you won't tell Hap who sent you here," he reminded the officers.

"Promise," they answered in unison.

"And you've got to hide me in the car, and lock the doors. He'll kill me if he gets his hands on me."

"You're safe with us, son," replied the driver. "You can lie on the floor and we'll cover you up. The doors will be locked. Don't worry, no one in their right mind will break into a police car in their own driveway."

"Yeah, but Hap is not in his right mind."

They continued to wind their way up the hillside.

"Turn left and this is his street," Alex directed. "It's the third house on the left. The one with the circular driveway. Stop here and cover me up. I don't want anyone to see me."

Alex felt rather than saw the cruiser pull into Hap's driveway.

"Breathe deep, Alex. We're going in now, but it shouldn't take long. If we find the boy we're going to have to arrest the occupants. We'll call for a backup in that case. Don't worry, you won't have to face him."

"Thanks," was the muffled reply.

Alex heard both car doors open and shut. Then it was still. He waited. And waited. His head pounded and his heart banged in his chest. He felt his legs stiffen up and begin to cramp, but there was no way he could move. He was sure Hap or one of his goons would be watching the car carefully for any sign of life.

Finally Alex felt sure something must have happened to the officers. Was Hap crazy enough to kill them both to protect himself? There was no way it would take this long to search the house.

The car door opened. Then the other door opened. Both doors shut. Alex remained still. The keys were put in the ignition and the car was started up. Alex felt it backing out of the driveway.

"It's just us, Alex," came the familiar voice of Constable Russell. "We'll tell you when we're around the corner and you can sit up."

Alex heaved a sigh of relief. "I thought maybe you were Hap hijacking the police cruiser."

Both officers laughed, though ruefully. "Sorry we didn't greet you sooner but your *friends* were watching us leave and we didn't want them to see us talking to an empty car. The coast is clear, you can sit up now."

Alex slowly stretched his cramped body into an upright position.

"So, what did you find?"

"Nothing, I'm afraid. And we searched every square inch of that house."

"Nothing!"

"Sorry, son. But there is no prisoner there. Which doesn't mean there wasn't one, though."

Alex sat in stunned silence. There was no doubt in his mind that Hap had abducted his look-alike, but where did he have him? Was he already dead?

"A pretty suspicious-looking lot, though. There's something illegal going on there. Drugs, more than likely."

"Then why didn't you arrest them?"

"For what? Looking suspicious?"

"I told you what they were doing."

"But you didn't know what you were delivering. Anyway, now that you've led us to them we can get a detective on the case. We have to catch them red-handed, doing whatever it is they do."

Alex sighed. "Now what?"

"Well, if it's okay with you, we'll take you back to the station to see what else you can tell us that might help us find Tanner."

As they crossed back over the bridge, Alex looked down at the gray water. He noticed the empty beaches that lined the shores. What else could he tell them? Hap, he thought, had probably already killed the boy and disposed of the body. The boy that was supposed to be him.

....

Back at the police station, Alex was led to a little room. There was a cot set up in one corner.

"You're looking a little rough, son. Thought you might like to lie down for awhile. You rest while we write up a report, and then someone will be back in to talk to you."

Alex just nodded. He really was exhausted. He was already lying down before the police officer had shut the door behind him.

He closed his eyes. His head was still pounding. He wondered if he would be able to sleep with such an intense headache.

Help me.

Alex's eyes flew open. There was that little voice again. But today it was weak, pleading. Could he have imagined it? He must have. He closed his eyes and tried to clear his head, but suddenly an image appeared in his mind — a very familiar-looking structure. He had never seen it from this angle before, but he certainly knew what it was. He forced his eyes to stay closed, to see if any other images would come to mind. But the same picture held fast. And once again he heard the voice.

Help me. Oh God, please help me.

Alex jumped up and raced out of the small room into the bustling hub of the police station.

"I know where he is," he yelled to no one in particular. Every head turned to look at him. Alex looked around frantically. He felt an urgency that he had never felt before. He saw Constable Russell get up from his desk and approach him.

"I know where he is. Can you take me there?"

"How do you know, son?"

"I just do. And we've got to hurry. He's in bad shape."

The officer just stared at him. He looked around at the group of police who had joined them. They all looked puzzled, but no one said anything.

The officer looked at his watch. "Listen, Alex, I'm due for my lunch break. I'll drive you there. This will be an off-duty thing. Is that okay with you?"

"Can we take the police car? We may need the radio."

"Sure."

"Okay, let's go then."

....

For the second time that day, Alex sat in a police car heading toward the Lions Gate Bridge. Fortunately there were two lanes heading north this time, so the traffic moved steadily.

"Which exit should I take?" the officer asked.

"I'm not quite sure. All I know is he is lying in the bush somewhere near this bridge."

Alex felt rather than saw the officer look at him.

"Could that be somewhere near Ambleside Beach?" the officer asked, gesturing to the park area that lay to the left of the bridge that they were now crossing.

Alex studied the park. There was a wooded area near the bridge that could easily be the place he was looking for. The other side of the bridge was an industrial park.

"Could be. Can you take me there?"

"You bet," said the officer, taking the West Vancouver exit once again. He drove along Marine Drive, heading west. Alex recognized the shopping center that Hap had taken him to. Then they pulled into the parking lot of the public beach area.

"This is as far as we can go by car, son," said the officer as he pulled into a parking stall. "Where to now?"

"We have to walk back toward the bridge."

"Then let's go."

As they headed east, Alex kept an eye on the bridge that loomed overhead. He felt his breath coming in shallow pants. Anxiety like he'd never known before consumed him. When the bridge looked just as it had in the image in his mind, he knew they were close. He stopped and looked around.

"He has to be right over there," Alex said, gesturing toward the treed area to their left.

"You sure?"

"Yeah. Hurry. Please!"

"Stay here then, son. I'll go investigate." Alex watched as the officer moved into the trees. Within seconds he squatted down to peer at something. Then Alex saw him remove his jacket and lay it down. He stood up and sprinted back to where Alex was waiting. He just nodded at Alex as he pulled his radio off his belt and turned it on.

"Requesting ambulance at Ambleside Park. East end, near the bridge." He clipped it back onto his belt.

"You found him," said Alex. It was a statement, not a question.

"Yes. He's in rough shape but he's alive. I'm going back there, but I want you to wait here to flag down the ambulance." He started back toward the trees then suddenly turned around.

"How did you know where to find him?"

Alex shrugged his shoulders. "I don't know."

"You'll have some explaining to do," the officer said gently.

Alex just nodded. He didn't care how it looked. He was just glad that they got here in time. He looked up and watched the stream of traffic crossing the bridge overhead.

twenty-three

Tanner opened his eyes and tried to focus. Although his vision was blurry, he guessed he was in a hospital by the medicinal smell in the room.

"Tanner!" his mother cried. "You're awake! It's us, honey, Dad and I."

"Hey, Mom," he croaked. He could see her now, leaning over him, her face just inches from his own.

"We're so relieved to see you, son." said his father, a tremble evident in his voice. "You gave us quite a scare."

"How long have I been here?" he asked, though it was hard to talk because his throat was incredibly dry.

"About twenty-four hours, give or take a few."

Tanner tried to concentrate. He remembered being snatched from Stanley Park and then taken to … a room, a room where … He forced himself not to think about it. But how did he get from there to here?

He tried to sit up. "Oh, man — I can't move."

"Lie still, honey," said his mom. "Just rest."

"How did I get here?" he asked.

"The police found you and brought you here," answered his mom. "You're going to be fine, honey. Be still." She ran her fingers through his hair, smoothing it out. He vaguely remembered someone else doing that, when he was in the room ...

The door opened and a nurse bustled in.

"Oh! The boy's come to, has he? Mom, Dad, could you step back while I take his vitals?"

Tanner lay still while the nurse recorded his temperature and pulse. He tried to get his bearings. If he was still in Vancouver, what were his parents doing here? And what had happened to Cara?

"Looking good, young man," said the nurse as she covered him up again. "You missed lunch, but I can have a tray sent up if you like."

"Great," answered Tanner.

"Good," she said. "Hunger's a good sign. What about pain? Do you need some painkillers?"

"Please."

"No problem," she answered. "And just push that button on the wall behind you if you need anything else. I'll let the doctor know you've come to. I'm sure he'll be in to see you soon." And with that she breezed back out the door.

"Am I still in Vancouver?" Tanner asked his parents.

"Yes. We flew in as soon as we heard ..." His mom couldn't bring herself to finish the sentence.

"I don't want to upset you, son, but can you tell us what happened? Why weren't you playing hockey with your team?"

"Well, I had ..."

To Tanner's relief, he didn't get to finish the sentence. The nurse was back in with some pain medication and a cup of water. She held his head forward while he sipped the water to wash down the pills.

"There's a whole crowd in the waiting room to see you,

Tanner," she said. "Are you up to any visitors? I told them they should come back later, but they won't leave."

"Yeah, sure," he answered, happy not to be left alone with his parents and their questions. He wasn't ready for that — not yet.

"I'll tell them to come in two at a time, and they each get only five minutes. In half an hour I'm sending security in to kick them all out so you can get some rest." Tanner noticed the twinkle in her eye. "You're some kind of folk hero you know," she added as she left.

So for the next half hour, Tanner welcomed a stream of teammates into his room. The tournament had been canceled after his abduction, so they were all restless and full of energy. Forgotten were the days leading up to the tournament when he'd been shunned because of his deteriorating hockey skills. They teased Tanner about his disfigured face, but they had obviously been cautioned not to ask about the events concerning his abduction. No one said a thing. They chatted about the tournament, hoping they could play some of the canceled games now that he was safe.

Jason hung around at the end of his five minutes. "I'm sorry about what I said, Tanner. I was just real worried about you."

"I know. I was being a jerk, too. I should have talked to you, tried to explain what was going on."

"You probably tried, but I wasn't listening."

"Whatever," said Tanner. "It's history now."

"Get better quick. We've got some catching up to do."

Tanner smiled, but his face was so distorted it looked more like a grimace.

"Man, you're ugly," Jason said with a grin. "I love it."

"There's one more person waiting to see you, Tanner," said Mr. Jack, who had supervised the visiting hockey players.

"But I don't know if you want her to see you looking like this. It might not do much for your love life, you know."

Tanner noticed his parents' eyebrows raise ever so slightly as they listened from their chairs in the corner of the hospital room. They had been timing the visitors, fearful that Tanner would get overtired.

"I'll take my chances," he answered, feeling his heart begin to race. It could only be one person.

He waited anxiously for her to come in. He saw the door open slowly and her face appear around the edge.

"Tanner?" she asked. He'd forgotten, for the moment, how disfigured his face was.

"Yeah, it's me. Come on in." His teammates had been fascinated by his injuries, but he could see the look of horror on Cara's face. "What did they do to you?" she asked, her eyes filling with tears.

"Hey, take it easy. I'm okay. It only hurts when I laugh ... or move." He smiled, painfully, knowing how grotesque he must look. "Cara, that's my mom and dad, hiding in the corner."

She turned and smiled, noticing them for the first time.

"We're going to go find a sandwich or something, Tanner," said his mom after greeting Cara. "We'll be back in a bit." His dad patted his shoulder gently before they left the room.

Cara couldn't contain the tears any longer. "I'm so sorry, Tanner. I felt so helpless — I couldn't stop them."

Tanner suddenly realized what an ordeal this must have been for her.

"Hey, I'm okay. Knock it off. There was nothing you could do." He watched as she reached for a tissue to blow her nose and wipe her eyes. He wished he could sit up and take her hand or even hug her, but he didn't dare move. He thought back to what they had been doing in the park when they were so suddenly interrupted. He felt himself blush and he looked away. She must have read his thoughts because she moved closer and gently picked up his hand.

"Do you know why it happened?" she asked.

Tanner felt a sudden wave of exhaustion come over him. "I think they mistook me for someone else. I don't remember much."

Tanner noticed the troubled look that crossed Cara's face just as the nurse came back into the room with a tray of food.

"Time to eat and rest, Tanner. No more visitors until this evening."

Cara got up. "Do you mind if I come back tonight, Tanner?"

"Can you stomach looking at me anymore?"

"It's not too bad, once you get used to it. I thought you were ugly anyway, remember?"

Tanner gritted his teeth. "I told you not to make me laugh — it hurts everywhere. See you tonight."

....

Tanner slept most of the afternoon and by 6:00 p.m., when the evening visiting hours began, he felt somewhat better. His vision was clearing and he could sit up now, propped by pillows. The doctor had been in to see him and didn't think there would be any permanent damage. He might have to see a physiotherapist to help him work on some of the muscle damage, but the more he moved around, the faster he would heal. The police had also been in but assured the hospital staff that they would refrain from asking too many questions until he had more of his strength back.

At 6:01 the door opened again and Cara poked her head around the corner.

Tanner's parents welcomed her in and they chatted for a little while, getting to know each other. Then the nurse came back in.

"Are you still here?" asked Tanner. "Don't they ever let you go home?"

"I'm just off, bud. End of a twelve-hour shift. Just wanted to check and see if you were up to any more visitors. There is a man and a boy asking to see you. They were here earlier, but I sent them away."

"Sure," said Tanner, though he felt a touch of resentment. He wished he could have Cara to himself for a while. He assumed it was someone from the team that he hadn't seen earlier. He wasn't prepared for who was about to walk into his hospital room.

twenty-four

After Tanner had been whisked away in the ambulance, Alex and the police officer had driven back to the city in silence. Finally, when they reached the parking lot outside the police station, the officer spoke.

"I'm afraid this looks rather strange, son," he said with a hand on Alex's shoulder. "How did you know where we would find him?"

"I really can't explain it," Alex answered with a sigh. "A vision of the bridge came into my mind and wouldn't leave. I heard a plea for help. I put the two together and, well, the rest is history."

The officer studied him for a few minutes. "Kind of like telepathy or something, eh?"

"Kind of, I guess."

"Well, Alex, I believe you, I really do. But I doubt anyone else will." They sat in silence for a few more minutes.

"We'll go in, write up a report, and then I'll take you back to your uncle's place. But that won't be the end of it, I'm afraid. You'll have a lot of explaining to do in the next few days."

....

At dinner that evening, Alex filled his uncle in on the details of the day. Suddenly the older man pushed his unfinished dinner aside.

"Damn it. I told your parents that they were making a big mistake — that it would backfire in their face someday!" He got up and started pacing about the kitchen. Alex watched him, confused and frightened.

"What are you talking about, Uncle John? What do my parents have to do with anything?"

"Don't you see what's happened, Alex? Haven't you figured out who Tanner is yet?" Alex's uncle stood behind the island in the middle of the kitchen. His hands were gripping the edge of the counter. Alex didn't know his tiny, soft-spoken uncle could show such emotion.

"No." A tingly feeling started in the pit of Alex's stomach and started working its way up to his throat. He couldn't bring himself to ask the obvious question — the one that was hanging in the air between them. Finally his uncle blurted it out.

"He's your twin brother, that's who!"

Alex and his uncle stared at each other. Alex's mind was blank. His uncle's words either weren't registering or he was refusing to hear them.

"I'm sorry, Alex. I didn't want to tell you like this, but it's got to come out in the open now." He sat back down across the table from Alex. All the rage was gone and he sat hunched over and deflated.

"How can I have a twin brother?" Alex's brain was beginning to work again.

"You were adopted, Alex. And you have a twin brother who was adopted by another family. At the time of your adoption I felt it was wrong to separate you two, but that's not the way your father felt about it. Your parents were first on the waiting list to adopt a baby, so they were given the choice of taking both of you or just one."

"And my father chose just one."

"Yes. Against everyone else's better judgment. Everyone except the adoption agency, that is."

"Why did they agree to separate us?"

"There was a great demand for babies. By separating you two, the needs of two families were met."

"Why didn't I know I was adopted?"

"Again, it was your father's doing. He didn't believe in telling you. That was about the time I started losing contact with your mother. I just couldn't understand why she didn't stand up to the man."

"She has now."

"Yes. Finally."

They sat in silence. After a while, Alex's uncle got up and started clearing away the plates.

"I'm sorry I had to tell you like this, Alex. It should have been your mother. But with all the events of the last few days, I just couldn't keep it to myself any longer." He studied Alex. "Are you okay, son?"

"Yeah. I'm exhausted though. I think I'll hit the sack"

"I'm sure you are. But Alex, please, as this information sinks in, come to me if you need to talk about it."

Alex thought he might have trouble sleeping that night. Being told he wasn't who he thought he was left him with a lot to ponder. But, fortunately, exhaustion won the battle and he had a deep, dreamless sleep.

....

Waking up early, Alex lay in bed and examined his feelings about being adopted. He expected to feel angry and deceived, but instead he felt as if a huge burden had been lifted from his chest. His mother still felt like his mother. She loved him wholeheartedly, and he knew it. But knowing his father was not a blood relation eased his guilt for the ambivalent feelings he had for him. Maybe it would be okay to hate his father after all. The man had certainly never acted like he loved him. Perhaps he'd never wanted to adopt a child in the first place. And this information cleared up so many uncertainties that had plagued him over the years. No wonder he often felt so different than the rest of his family.

And he had a twin brother! He had hated being an only child. He'd always had imaginary siblings when he was little. It was strange to think that someone identical to him had been living a separate life for fourteen years.

Alex leapt out of bed. He had to meet his twin. After dressing, he found his uncle emptying the dishwasher. The smell of frying bacon filled the kitchen.

"I want to go meet Tanner, Uncle John!"

Alex's uncle looked at his nephew in surprise. "Well good morning to you, too, Alex. You look like a new kid this morning."

"I feel great. And I can't wait to meet my brother."

"Well, slow down a second there, son. Let's have our breakfast and think about this thing."

"What's there to discuss, Uncle John? I've gone fourteen years without knowing my brother and I don't want to waste another day."

Alex's uncle passed him a plate. "Your mom should be arriving today."

"Don't change the subject."

"Well, let's consider the ramifications of you just suddenly showing up in this boy's hospital room. He probably doesn't know you exist. He might not even know he was adopted. His parents are probably with him, and they might be shocked to see you waltz in. And another thing, you said this boy was badly beaten. Meeting you right now might not be the best thing for his recovery."

"I don't care."

"And then he's going to find out that it was you who was supposed to get the beating, not him. How do you think he's going to feel about that?"

That stumped Alex. He ate his breakfast in silence.

"What about your mom? That you know about the adoption is going to be a shock to her. It's hard to say how she's going to react."

"Hmmm." Alex was still thinking about Tanner. He felt sure Tanner would be just as anxious to meet him as he was to meet Tanner.

"Have you thought about how you're going to break the news of the last three months to her? You're probably not the same small-town boy you were when you left Tahsis."

"Tanner may have taken the beating for me, but at least I led the police to him."

Alex's uncle laughed. "I see you have a one-track mind. We're talking about your mother."

"No. You're talking about my mother. I'm talking about my brother."

"Seriously, Alex. You've got to take this slow. When your mom gets here tonight, we'll talk to her about it then. See how she feels about you meeting your brother."

So Alex dropped the subject, for a few hours, anyway. After doing the breakfast dishes he excused himself and went for a walk. But the more he thought about it, the more anxious he was to see Tanner before he saw his mother. She might get very emotional and dampen his determination. She might make him feel guilty for even wanting to meet his brother. By the time he had returned to his uncle's, he had made up his mind. He found his uncle reading the paper in the living room.

"Uncle John, I'm going to the hospital to meet my brother. Are you coming with me or am I going alone?"

His uncle put the paper down with a sigh. "This is not how I expected you to react to the news of your adoption, Alex. But, very well, if I can't stop you I guess I'll have to join you."

Unfortunately, Alex was forced to wait a little longer. When they got to the hospital, the head nurse was adamant.

"Tanner's had too many visitors already today. He's resting now. Visiting hours start at 6:00 p.m. You can see him then."

twenty-five

The boy standing at the door was his spitting image. Tanner squeezed his eyes shut, wondering if he could be hallucinating. Maybe the combination of painkillers and antibiotics was doing things to his mind. But when he opened them again, the boy was still there.

"Alex!" gasped Cara.

So, thought Tanner, this is Cara's runaway boyfriend. No wonder she thought she had found him the other night at the Rec Center.

"What are you doing here, Cara?" asked Alex. Forgotten, momentarily, were the plans to meet his twin. Alex couldn't believe his eyes. This was getting even weirder.

"I met Tanner a few days ago … I thought he was you." They stared at each other, still trying to get over the shock of meeting in such an unlikely place. "What are you doing here?"

"Well …" He finally looked at the boy lying in the hospital bed. Then he looked at the couple sitting beside the bed. They must be Tanner's parents. They still wore expressions of complete shock at seeing Alex. Neither of them had moved or uttered a word. Tanner's face was a mess. Alex's stomach flipped when he realized that it was his own face that was supposed to look like that. "I've come to meet Tanner."

"How do you know anything about Tanner?" asked Cara.

"It was me that was supposed to be abducted in the park the other day," he answered. "I read about him in the paper." He glanced at his uncle who was leaning against the wall beside him. His uncle nodded, giving him moral support when he suddenly felt like turning and racing out of the room.

"You? But why?"

Alex sighed. "It's a long story, Cara. I'll tell you about it later. But I wanted to come and talk to Tanner, to tell him I'm sorry." He turned to the mangled face. "I guess you've gathered my name is Alex, and I'm the one who got you into this mess."

There was no response from Tanner or his parents. They just stared at him.

"Perhaps you'll forgive me a little if I tell you that I'm also the one who led the police to your unconscious body that had been dumped at Ambleside Park."

Alex noticed Tanner's eyebrows raise slightly. Tanner's father finally found his voice.

"How did you know where to find Tanner?"

"That's another story," answered Alex. It suddenly occurred to him that Tanner's parents might not appreciate him blurting out the news that he was Tanner's twin brother. Once again he looked to his uncle for support. His uncle came to Alex's rescue.

"If you'll excuse me for interrupting for a minute, I'm Alex's uncle, John Bradshaw. Alex has been staying with me for the last few days, when all this business of Tanner's abduction and so on was taking place." He shuffled forward and reached out to shake Tanner's parents' hands. They shook his hand, but unenthusiastically. "I was wondering if you'd step

out to the waiting room and allow me to chat with you a moment. There is a matter that I think you had better be informed
about."

The Boltons' eyebrows all raised in unison. Finally they
glanced at each other and then nodded slightly at Alex's uncle.

"I'd like to speak to you for a moment, too, son," he said to
Alex. So Alex and the Boltons followed Alex's uncle into the
hospital corridor. The Boltons held hands as they walked toward the waiting room.

"Just make small talk until we get back, Alex," Uncle John
whispered. "If Tanner doesn't know he's adopted, it's his parents' responsibility to tell him."

Alex nodded, then watched his uncle follow the Boltons
down the long hallway. He took a deep breath and pushed
open the door to Tanner's room. He noticed Cara had pulled
a chair up to the bed and was talking quietly to Tanner. He
felt a pang of jealousy but tried to push it down.

"So how are you, Cara? And what are you doing in Vancouver?"

"I'm okay. I'm in town with my family to visit Derek and
his family over the Christmas break. Remember him?"

Alex nodded.

"Have you talked to your mom?" she asked.

"Yeah, a couple days ago. She's coming into town tonight,
actually." He thought about the note they had left on the door
for her, telling her to get the key from the neighbors. He felt
bad that they wouldn't be there to welcome her, but this was
more important right now. "She told me about my dad."

Tanner watched the exchange between the other two. He
could feel the uneasiness in their conversation.

"I'm sorry."

"I'm not. He's a jerk. She'll be way better off without him.
Me too, for that matter."

"I hadn't heard from you in a while. I was getting pretty worried."

"I didn't call 'cause I had no good news to report. I hit rock bottom, actually."

"Oh Alex, I'm sorry."

"That's how I got mixed up with Hap and his crowd. I didn't realize what I was getting into, but I was desperate, and they offered me some hope."

"Hap's the guy who did this?" asked Tanner, pointing to his face.

Alex closed his eyes and nodded. "I can't tell you how sorry I am." He opened his eyes. "I'm surprised he didn't kill you, actually. There's something to be thankful for."

"What were you doing for this Hap guy?" asked Cara.

"Nothing. I had only known him for one day. He pumped me full of beer and bought me some new clothes. Then he assumed I'd work for him."

"And did you?"

"No! He gave me a parcel and told me to deliver it to the airport. I jumped out of the car in Stanley Park." Alex noticed the look that passed between Cara and Tanner. He felt the little pang of jealousy again but continued. "His thug had a gun and fired at me but I got away. It was the next day, Tanner, that you got nabbed. They obviously thought they had me. Who would have guessed that my double would be in the park the very next day!"

There was a long silence in the room. No one looked at each other. Alex finally decided to take the bull by the horns.

"So, what were you guys doing in Stanley Park, in December of all months?"

Tanner and Cara looked at each other, wondering who would reply. Finally Cara spoke up.

"I met Tanner at my cousin's hockey tournament. Like I

said ... I thought he was you at first. But he convinced me that he wasn't. Anyway, we got to talking and he told me how badly he wanted to see the ocean. He'd never been to the coast before. He wasn't playing hockey that day so we decided to go for a walk around the seawall. And that's when it happened."

The door opened and the adults came back into the room. Alex studied Mrs. Bolton's face. She'd obviously been crying, but she looked composed now. Cara got up and gave her the chair beside the bed. Mrs. Bolton sat down and picked up her son's hand. Mr. Bolton sat on the other side of the bed.

"Tanner, there is something we need to discuss," began Mr. Bolton.

"Excuse me for interrupting, but perhaps you would like us to leave?" asked Alex's uncle.

Mr. Bolton glanced at his wife and she smiled and shook her head.

"No, this is a family matter, and you're family now, right?"

Mr. Bradshaw smiled warmly. "Thank you. I'm honored."

Tanner watched the adults, puzzled. He looked at Cara. She shrugged, equally confused.

"You see, Tanner," continued his father. "There is something we should have told you years ago. We always meant to, but the time never seemed just right. Then it seemed we'd waited too long so we decided there was no point. Anyway, as it turns out, we should have told you, because something very unexpected has come up."

"Could you get to the point, Dad," said Tanner.

"Tanner ... " started his mom. "You see ... well ..."

"You're adopted, son," said his dad. Alex watched Tanner's face. It was only last night that he'd been given the same amazing news, and he knew what a shock it was.

"I'm sorry, honey," sniffled his mom. "We should have told you a long time ago. But the truth is we never even think about it. You're our son, no matter how you came into our lives. But you have a right to know the truth."

Mr. Bolton wiped his eyes. "We love you, Tanner, and nothing will ever change that. I'm sorry if this is a shock to you."

Tanner looked from his mom to his dad. "You know," he said, "this doesn't really surprise me. I always knew that I looked different than everyone else." He looked at his anguished parents. "Hey, don't beat yourself up about this. I'm okay with it. I really am. I always had a feeling I was different. But what did you mean when you said something unexpected turned up?"

His parents glanced at each other. Mr. Bolton nodded.

"You were just a few days old when we were notified that a baby had been born that we could adopt. We rushed to Vancouver to get you. The social worker had given us a package of papers describing your history and so on, but we asked her not to tell us too much. You were our son already, and we didn't want to think of you any other way. We decided to seal the envelope of papers and put them into the safety deposit box to give to you when you turned nineteen or when you expressed a strong interest in your history. You see, we really did mean to tell you the truth. Anyway, because we didn't read the information ourselves, we didn't know that you were actually one of a set of twins — identical twins."

Tanner stared at his mom. "You mean ..." he pointed at Alex.

"That's right, honey. He must be your twin. Nobody else could look so much like you. And Alex's Uncle John knew that Alex was separated from a twin.

Tanner and Alex stared at each other.

"If it helps any, I just found out about the adoption thing last night," Alex said. "This news is almost as new to me as it is to you."

"Unbelievable," said Cara, shaking her head. "I should have guessed."

"That's true," Alex said. "You're the only one who had met both of us before today."

Tanner had remained silent, trying to absorb the news. Finally he smiled.

"Who would have guessed that I'd have to get beaten to a pulp to meet my long-lost brother." He reached out a bandaged hand. "Good to meet you, Alex. I've always wanted a brother."

"Me too," said Alex, not trying to mask the tears in his eyes.

twenty-six

The sunshine that poured in through the hospital window felt warm on the skin.

"Only on the coast can it feel like spring in the dead of winter," commented Mr. Bolton from beside his son's hospital bed. "Maybe we should think about moving here," he mused, looking at his wife.

"Yeah," answered Tanner and Alex in unison. Now that they had found each other they weren't looking forward to going their separate ways again.

"And give up having a white Christmas? I don't think so," she answered. But she knew how difficult it was going to be for the boys to say good-bye. In just a couple of days they had become very close. Alex had spent every waking minute at Tanner's bedside in the hospital. The adults had given them a lot of time to get to know each other when they realized how well they had clicked.

Saying good-bye to Cara had been awkward, but the boys were so absorbed in each other that they hadn't dwelled on it. They would both write to her, and she had promised to keep in touch with them.

Alex would be staying in Vancouver with his mom and Uncle John. Alex's mom had been shocked but relieved to discover that her son had met his twin brother. She had never been happy keeping it a secret from him and was relieved that the responsibility of informing him had been taken out of her hands.

"We're going to go for a walk to get some fresh air," said Mrs. Bolton. "Can we bring you a sandwich or something when we come back, Alex?"

"Yeah, that would be great, thanks," he replied.

"Me too," said Tanner. "One more hospital meal and I think I really might die!"

"No way, son," said Mr. Bolton. "We're saving a small fortune with the hospital feeding you. We have to take advantage of it while we can. In a couple days you'll be back to eating us out of house and home again."

"Oh, man," groaned Tanner, watching his parents leave. "Want to exchange lunches today, Alex?"

Alex ignored the question. Now that the Boltons were gone, they could get back to work. He closed his eyes. "Okay ... give me a sec, give me a sec. There. What am I sending?"

Tanner closed his eyes, too. He let his mind go completely blank. Suddenly an image of a black and hairy gorilla jumped into his head.

"Hey! I see you!" he teased.

"Very funny," replied Alex. "What do you see?"

"King Kong," he answered.

"Good," said Alex. "Your turn. Send me something."

The twins had discovered their ability when Alex was telling Tanner of his dilemma with the police. He hadn't been able to convince them that a mental image of the Lions Gate Bridge had led him to his twin's body. Tanner listened to Alex's story in amazement.

"I kept coming to and seeing that bridge," he explained to Alex. "I couldn't move so I tried screaming for help, but my throat was so dry I don't think anything came out. It was horrible."

Alex was fascinated. "I must have received a mental image from you," he said.

"Do you really think so?" asked Tanner.

"Let's try it."

And so their unique gift had been discovered. The police had come to Tanner's room and listened to their explanation. They looked skeptical but decided to accept the theory for lack of any other rational one. They were easily convinced that Alex wasn't working with Hap. Then they told Alex that a witness had stepped forward and had given enough evidence against Hap that he had been arrested.

"What will happen to the witness?" asked Alex, suspecting he knew who she was.

"Don't worry about her, son," Officer Russell had said. "She'll be given a very light sentence because she came forward on her own accord." He winked at Alex. "She says to say hi," he whispered.

Alex blushed. He was glad Maureen had busted Hap. He hoped she would be able to straighten out her own life.

"You know, I was thinking, Alex," said Tanner.

"Oh no, not again," replied Alex. "We don't want you to strain yourself."

"Shut up and listen," said Tanner. "I think I've been receiving messages from you for quite some time now, only you didn't know you were sending them and I didn't know what they were."

"How so?"

"I've had this recurring dream. There is this person I need to escape from. I am swimming away, actually."

"My father," said Alex, quietly.

"But lately I'd felt like I was drowning and I almost gave

up a few times in my dreams."

"That pretty much sums up my life in the last few months."

"Whoa. I hope I don't have to experience your life in my dreams forever."

Alex thought about it. "Well, now that my father's out of my life, maybe I won't be sending such distress signals." He paused. "Maybe we'll always know when the other is experiencing stress. Unless we can learn to block the messages somehow."

"Speaking of distress signals, there is something else I've discovered I can do when I'm totally steamed," said Tanner.

"What's that?"

"Move things." Tanner watched Alex's face for the reaction. He expected to see disbelief or laughter, but all he saw was curiosity. Now that they knew they could pass images to each other telepathically, anything was possible.

"Show me."

"Well, I have to be really ticked or be thinking really angry thoughts. It takes a lot of concentration, and then I'm exhausted. But when it works, watch out — you never know what may come crashing down."

"Are you going to show me?"

"That's what I was getting at. I'm not sure if I'm up to the effort yet. But I'll try." He glanced around the hospital room, wondering what would be affected. "Okay, watch out." He closed his eyes and thought of Hap. It was the first time he had allowed himself to think of him since he had woken up in the hospital. He remembered the way Hap had berated him for running away and then began to kick him. The more Tanner screamed for mercy, pleading that he had never met Hap before, the harder the blows became. The more he kicked, the angrier Hap seemed to become. Tanner could feel himself beginning to shake. It was too horrible. He didn't want to remember it. He opened his eyes just as a picture came crashing down off the wall behind Alex. The glass shattered on the hard floor. The swinging door to the hall began to move, but no one came in. Alex's eyes widened, taking in the effects of Tanner's concentration. Then he noticed Tanner blinking back tears.

"Hey, man, I'm sorry. I didn't mean to upset you."

"I was thinking of Hap." Tanner sniffed. "I had put him out of my mind until now, but I guess I had to deal with it sooner or later."

The door opened and Tanner's parents came back into the room. Their glance took in the smashed picture on the floor and Tanner wiping his eyes.

"What's happening here, boys?" asked Mr. Bolton.

"I don't know. The picture fell suddenly. I was just telling Alex about Hap. I'm okay."

"Take it easy, son. Everything's okay now. That animal is behind bars." Tanner's dad pulled a couple of oblong packages out of the bag he was holding. "This will cheer you up. We took pity on you after all. We brought you a cold cut sub — with the works. Extra hot sauce, too."

Alex thought about what he had just witnessed as he munched on his sandwich. He wondered if he had the same ability. He also wondered if he wanted it.

....

Two months later Alex picked up the phone and dialed Tanner's number in Edmonton.

"Did you get anything?" he asked.

"An image? No. But I got a letter from Cara," Tanner answered.

"Me too. A Dear John letter, right?"

"Yeah. I feel kinda bad. I guess I messed things up between you two, eh?"

"You got that right," agreed Alex. He thought sadly of

158 ...... *Shelley Hrdlitschka*

their parting words last fall — how she vowed she'd wait for him, "as long as it takes."

"But I guess it wasn't meant to be," he continued. "I have no intention of moving back to Tahsis, and she loves it there. Not much future in that, is there?"

"No, I guess not."

"And besides, like she said, if the three of us were together, I would always be wondering if there was something going on between you two."

"A person can't help their feelings."

"That's true. That's why it's time to close that chapter and move on.

"Good. I'm glad you're not taking it too hard. I only knew her for a few days, so it's not such a big deal. Wish I could meet someone else like her, though."

"Me too. Anyway, you haven't received any of my thought messages, have you?"

"Not a one. You?"

"No. It must be the distance that makes it harder, but I'm not giving up. You have to concentrate on tuning in."

"I'll keep listening, so to speak. And you keep sending. After all, I received your thoughts in my dreams last fall, no problem. We know it can be done."

"Yeah, and when I come to Edmonton on spring break, I want some more instructions on how to move things. I haven't been able to pull that off yet either."

"I'll give you a hint. Get mad — real mad."

"I'll try. I better go. Mom's threatening to make me start paying for these phone calls."

"Hey. It's worth it."

"I know. And Tanner?"

"Yeah?"

"Stay tuned."

.... epilogue

Alex lay on his bed in his uncle's house, thinking of the conversation he had just had with his father on the phone.

"C'mon, Alex. Come home," he'd begged. "I'm changed, you'll see. I'll never hurt you again. I need you and your mom. I'm nobody without my family."

"We're staying here," was the sullen reply.

"You get your butt on the next ferry and get home." Alex wasn't surprised at the sudden change in his father's tone. He'd heard it all before. "And if you're not home by tomorrow night I'm coming there to get you. Then you'll be sorry. You'll wish you'd obeyed your old man and that you'd never stolen a nickel from me. I mean it, Alex. I'll have you screaming for mercy."

Alex noticed that his words were even more slurred than usual tonight. He knew it was just the alcohol talking, but these calls really upset his mother. He knew she feared his father, and he and his Uncle John had trouble comforting her. That his father was still able to hurt her infuriated Alex. He'd like to get his hands around his father's throat and …

Alex noticed the trophy that his mother had brought to

him from Tahsis — the same trophy that he had stored his stolen money in — begin to tremble where it stood on the book case. Suddenly it flipped and landed on the floor beside the bed.

Alex stared at it in disbelief. I did it, he thought. I really did it!

....

Tanner was sitting at his desk trying to concentrate on his homework, but images from the swimming dream kept creeping into his mind. He hadn't had the dream since his trip to Vancouver, so he was surprised to find himself thinking of it again. Suddenly an image of a large gold trophy popped into his head. Where, he thought, did that come from?

A moment later the phone rang. Instantly he knew who it would be. They had done it. They had finally connected — long distance.

---

author's note

In the area of psi phenomena, psychokinesis is the ability of mind over matter. It has been observed that teens, who are often greatly affected by their feelings, can become so troubled by a problem that their emotions build up into a kind of vibration. This vibration has been known to leave their bodies and move whatever it strikes. Sometimes it happens over and over again until the problem is resolved.